"I'm in need of a wife."

The statement was made so nonchalantly that Victoria wondered if she had heard Antonio correctly. "Sorry did you say…a wife?"

He smiled. "Don't look so worried—this is a marriage for business purposes only."

Victoria shook her head and tried to gather her senses from the fragmented emotions whirling inside her. She knew full well that Antonio Cavelli could have any woman he pleased. "So… run this by me again. Why exactly do you need a wife? And why are you asking me to do this?"

"I'm asking you because you're convenient. I'm in need of a ready-made family for a short-term period without any strings or complications. You will do nicely." He reached for the calendar on his desk. "It's a case of being in the right place at the right time," he added with a smile as he flicked through the pages.

"Lucky me, then." Her voice was low and tight as she fought to suppress the anger rising inside her….

KATHRYN ROSS was born in Zambia to an English father and an Irish mother. She was educated in Ireland and England, where she later worked as a professional beauty therapist before becoming a full-time writer.

Most of her childhood was spent in a small village in southern Ireland; she said it was a wonderful place to grow up, surrounded by the spectacular beauty of the Wicklow Mountains and the rugged coastline of the Irish Sea. She feels that living in Ireland first sparked her desire to write; it was so rich in both scenery and warm characters that it literally invited her to put pen to paper.

Kathryn doesn't remember a time when she wasn't scribbling. As a child she wrote adventure stories and a one-act play that won a competition. She became editor of her school magazine, which she said gave her great training for working into the night and meeting deadlines. Happily, ten years later Harlequin Books accepted her first book, *Designed with Love*, for publication.

Kathryn loves to travel and seek out exotic locations for her books. She feels it helps her writing to be able to set her scenes against backgrounds that she has visited. Also, traveling and meeting people give her great inspiration. That's how all her novels start—she gets a spark of excitement from some incident or conversation and that sets her imagination working. Her characters are always a pastiche of different people she has either met or read about, or would like to meet. She likes being a novelist because she can make things happen—well, most of the time anyhow. Sometimes her characters take over and do things that surprise even her!

At present Kathryn is working on her thirty-first book, and can be found walking her dogs in the Lake District as she thinks about her plots.

ITALIAN MARRIAGE:
IN NAME ONLY
KATHRYN ROSS

~ RUTHLESS TYCOONS ~

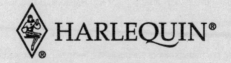

TORONTO • NEW YORK • LONDON
AMSTERDAM • PARIS • SYDNEY • HAMBURG
STOCKHOLM • ATHENS • TOKYO • MILAN • MADRID
PRAGUE • WARSAW • BUDAPEST • AUCKLAND

Recycling programs
for this product may
not exist in your area.

ISBN-13: 978-0-373-52764-9

ITALIAN MARRIAGE: IN NAME ONLY

First North American Publication 2010.

Copyright © 2010 by Kathryn Ross.

ITALIAN MARRIAGE: IN NAME ONLY

CHAPTER ONE

'SO WHAT'S the script on this place?' Antonio Cavelli asked his accountant as the limousine pulled up outside the glass-fronted restaurant.

Tom Roberts referred to his notes. 'We purchased the building last summer, the leaseholder is one Victoria Heart. So far she has turned down two offers from us to buy her out, so we've increased her rent. She's now struggling to remain open. So I think she'll sign on the dotted line this time.'

Antonio frowned. He'd just flown in from his office in Verona, and he'd only been in Australia for a few hours but already he was questioning Tom's handling of his business. 'This should have been a straightforward purchase,' he growled. 'And we are now six months down the line—what are you playing at?'

The accountant's face turned an interesting shade of purple and he brushed a hand nervously through his thinning hair. 'It's all under control, I assure you,' he muttered nervously. 'We've had a few problems, I know…but…'

Antonio's mobile phone rang and he halted Tom's stuttering apologies midsentence as he saw that it was his lawyer on the line. Right now he had more pressing problems than the simple takeover of an insignificant little restaurant. Right now the whole future of his company was hanging in the balance, as his father attempted to play out the most bizarre and ridiculous charade in order to bend him to his will.

Antonio's mouth tightened in an angry line. Nobody told him what to do, he thought as he snapped open the phone. *Nobody*—least of all the one man in the world for whom he felt nothing but contempt.

'Ricardo, have you got good news for me?' He switched to his native Italian language as he addressed his lawyer.

The silence at the other end of the line was answer enough.

'I've been through all our options a million times, Antonio,' the lawyer said finally, his voice heavy with regret. 'And there's not much we can do. We could take him to court—human rights, and all. But in my opinion all that's going to do is make for one hell of a media splash. You'll be sensationalizing the family's personal business, opening up the rift between you and your father for the world's scrutiny, and at the end of the day we probably won't win. The fact of the matter is that you may have built up the company into the success story it is today, but your father still owns sixty percent of Cavelli Enterprises. It's his to do what he wants with.'

Antonio's dark eyes flared with fire. He didn't care if the entire world knew what he thought of his father, but he did care that it would be opening up his mother's name to the humiliation of the past—and he couldn't do that. She'd suffered enough at the hands of his father already. Her memory should be left with dignity.

So how should he handle this? As Antonio's anger simmered, his sharp business mind kicked in to look for an answer. He wasn't going to allow his father to win this battle. Luc Cavelli may be the chairman of the company but he was a mere figurehead these days—Antonio was the brain, the one who had turned his father's provincial chain of Italian hotels into a global success story. He smiled to himself, because he had done so very much against his father's will. Luc hadn't wanted to expand the company—he had liked being a big fish in a small pond, able to control and manipulate everyone. But Antonio had forced his hand when he'd inherited his mother's shares, had dragged the company forward and had enjoyed doing it—had enjoyed seeing his father get further and further out of his depth until he was floundering.

So what now? He could call his father's bluff, sell his forty percent and walk away, leaving the old man to follow through with his threat and sell off the rest of the company. He would find it wasn't worth as much without him at the helm, anyway. But why should he, he thought furiously, when he had put so many years of his life into building it all up? 'There will be a way around this.' He spoke in a low tone, almost to himself.

'Well, if there is I can't see it. I've read your father's correspondence to you and the bottom line, Antonio, is that if you are not married and have not produced a child by the time you are thirty-five your father will sell his shares. He thinks that, as you are his only son, you have a duty to ensure the future of the Cavelli family. He also says that he wants to see you happily settled down.'

A curl of contempt swirled inside of Antonio. What a hypocrite! This was the man who had walked out on him and his mother when he'd been just ten years of age. He hadn't given a damn about family commitment back then, had been too busy humiliating his wife by parading his string of mistresses in public.

'He seems very determined,' his lawyer added softly.

'Yes, well, not as determined as I am to thwart him.'

'Hmm…' There was a moment's silence. 'The good news is that if you do comply with his wishes he will immediately sign over all of his shares in the company to you. I have it in writing.'

'Have you now…' A cold hard resolve closed around Antonio's heart. OK, if his father wanted to play these games, then he would rise to the challenge. But he would not allow him to win. He would find a way around this and gain control of everything—and then he would make him regret the day and hour he had tried to dictate terms to him. 'And I will be pleased to take control of his shares, but not by doing exactly as he wants.'

'Well, I can't see any other way around it. Your father wants you to get married and produce a child. And, in effect, he's served notice on you. Given you two years.'

'There is a solution to every problem Ricardo. Email or fax me with the relevant documentation so that I can see exactly what he has put in writing, and I'll speak to you later.' Antonio hung up and looked across at the man sitting opposite. 'So where were we…?' he enquired, switching to perfect English as he compartmentalized the problem of his father and focused on the business at hand.

Tom looked at him warily. He hadn't understood a word his boss had just said but he'd seen the anger in his eyes and he knew he should now tread very carefully. Antonio Cavelli had a reputation for being fair in business but also a reputation for being ruthless when it came to getting rid of people who didn't attain his high standards or displeased him in any way. 'I…I was just saying that I will sort the purchase of the restaurant out—'

'Ah, yes,' Antonio cut across him. 'This is dragging on too long, Tom. And frankly I'm starting to question your handling of the situation.'

'Sir, I realize this is taking longer than you would want but I assure you I am handling the matter in the best way possible.' The accountant shifted earnestly forward on the leather seat. 'For instance, I've made sure that Ms Heart doesn't realize your involvement or interest in her business. I've used your subsidiary company, Lancier, for all communications with her.'

'What's the point of that?' Antonio's eyes narrowed. 'I don't do business by the back door, Tom.'

'I can assure you that this is all perfectly legal and above board!' The man sat up straight now. 'What I have managed to do is keep the price down for you, as she has no idea of the strategic importance her building has for us.'

'Just increase the offer, Tom, and wrap the deal up,' Antonio told him dismissively. He had more important matters to deal with than this.

'With respect, sir, we don't need to increase the offer. I think Ms Heart's reticence to sell has been down to the fact that she is emotionally attached to her business—oh, and she's worried about her staff losing their jobs.'

'Well, then, arrange for their redeployment somewhere else within my company. I'm opening a new hotel next door to her, for heaven's sakes. I'll leave it with you.' Antonio picked up his briefcase and reached for the door handle. 'Meanwhile I'll take lunch here.'

'Here?' Tom looked startled.

'Why not, it looks like a fairly decent restaurant and I'm right outside it. I suggest you go back to the office, crunch numbers and finalize the agreement this afternoon.'

The heat of the street hit Antonio like warm nectar after the air-conditioned cool of the car. It was pleasant to be outside after the long flight from Europe, pleasant to be away from Tom Roberts. The guy really was a barracuda. But then that was why he was employing him, Antonio reminded himself sharply. He needed men on the ground at each location overseeing things. Tom was his man in Sydney. His remit was to keep the company lean, mean and able to survive the tough economic climate. And on the whole he was doing a good job. They had expanded down under; this was their tenth hotel on the Australasian continent. However, the man did need reining in—he seemed to enjoy the power trip of his position too much at times.

Antonio took his time and strolled across the wide pavement, taking in the aspects of the restaurant. Ms Heart certainly had picked herself a good location; the restaurant was on a main road beside a small leafy park, yet close enough to the sea to have sweeping views of it from the upstairs terrace. Pity it happened to be practically tagged onto the side of the building he had just purchased. If he raised his head he could see the new Cavelli hotel towering behind her restaurant, taking up more than two blocks of the Sydney street. He was having the place completely remodelled with no expense spared. The Cavelli name was synonymous with luxury and elegance and it was already booked out ahead of the doors opening in two months' time.

Ms Heart was literally a thorn in his side. Her restaurant had to go to make way for some designer boutiques and a new side entrance.

As he entered the main reception area he noticed with some surprise the polished wooden floors and the pale sofas strategically placed to overlook the greenery of the park. Ms Heart had good taste; the layout and design was impressive. And from what he could see the main body of the restaurant was fairly busy, with a clientele that seemed to consist mainly of business people taking lunch. But there were a few spare tables.

There was no one behind the reception desk and he was about to go straight through to the restaurant when the door behind the desk opened and a young woman came out. She had a pile of files in one hand, a pen in the other and looked as if she were deep in contemplation.

'Good afternoon, sir, can I help you?' She asked the question distractedly without looking over at him as she put the files down.

'Yes, I'd like a table for lunch.'

'How many for?' Still she didn't look at him; she seemed to be searching for something amongst the files.

'Just for one.' His gaze moved slowly over her. He guessed she was in her early twenties but the dark suit she wore was more the preserve of an older woman and did nothing for her slender figure, whilst the white blouse beneath was buttoned securely up to the neck.

She looked rather like an old-fashioned schoolmarm, or a librarian from the early nineteenth century, he thought with amusement. Her long dark hair was swept severely back from her face and secured into a tight chignon, and she was wearing dark-rimmed spectacles that seemed too heavy for her small face.

Victoria found the file she was looking for and glanced up, intercepting his detailed critical analysis of her appearance. And suddenly she found herself blushing.

She'd already decided he was Italian with an accent that was bone-meltingly sexy, but the fact that he was also incredibly attractive made her feel even more acutely embarrassed. Why was he looking at her like that? How dare he!

'So do you think you could fit me in?' he asked nonchalantly.

'Maybe…just one second and I'll take a look.' She knew very well that she had several spare tables. But it didn't do any harm to bluff a little. 'Yes…' She traced an imaginary line in her appointments book. 'Yes, you are in luck.'

He looked amused at that. And she had the feeling that he knew very well that she hadn't really needed to consult the book.

He was very irritating, she decided vehemently. And those bold, piercing dark eyes of his were unnerving her completely.

OK, he was probably the most handsome man she had ever set eyes on—*but didn't he just know it*. The suit he was wearing looked designer and expensive and he had the most perfect, powerful physique.

Quickly she pulled herself together; she didn't want to give him the satisfaction of thinking that she was interested in him, because she wasn't. He was well out of her league— a man like him would only date the world's most beautiful women and that certainly wasn't her.

But anyway, she had more important things to think about—namely, trying to save her restaurant. She had a meeting with her bank in an hour and she needed to be able to convince them that she could ride out this recession, otherwise…well…otherwise she could lose everything.

'I'll get someone to show you to your table.' Hastily she

looked around for her receptionist, Emma, but she was nowhere in sight.

Where was she? Victoria wondered anxiously. She really didn't want to leave the security of the desk. There was something about the way this man was looking at her that was making her unbearably self-conscious.

Their eyes clashed across the counter. 'Sorry about this—won't be a minute.'

'Perhaps you should show me to the table,' he said briskly. 'I'm on a tight schedule.'

'Oh…yes, of course.' Annoyed with herself for being so pathetic, Victoria tipped her chin up and moved. She didn't know what was wrong with her. One of her strengths was that she had good people skills. She dealt with customers every day without a bother; in fact, her regular clientele loved it when she was front of house because she always remembered them and was able to engage them in conversations about themselves.

Antonio watched as she walked around from behind the desk and then led him through the busy restaurant. She was wearing flat heels that did nothing for her. But she did have nice ankles, he noticed, and her legs looked decent enough… well, the little he could see of them. His eyes moved upwards over her body. It wasn't that she looked a mess, because she didn't; in fact, she was smartly dressed. It was just that she was—what was the word for it?—*staid*, yes, that was it. For a young woman she was definitely staid. It was as if she were afraid that a man might look at her in any way that was sexual.

The notion intrigued him.

As she turned to pull out a chair for him she caught the way he was looking at her and immediately a red-hot wave of embarrassment seared through her. She'd imagined she could feel his eyes on her, assessing her from top to toe as they walked through the restaurant, but she'd told herself not to be silly. Now she was sure he had been looking at her, weighing her up with that gleam in his dark eyes as if she were some sub-species worthy of amusement.

Obviously he thought she was a real plain Jane. Not that she cared whether he found her attractive or not. She didn't have time for such things, but strangely it still hurt.

'I'll get a waitress to take your order,' she mumbled.

'No.' He detained her before she could move away, his manner firm, as if he were used to issuing orders and having them obeyed. 'As I said, I'm in a hurry. So you can take my order.'

She watched as he reached for the menu that was sitting on the table. Part of her wanted to just walk away and ignore the command. But for the sake of good customer relations the sensible side of her wouldn't allow it. 'OK…' She tried to snap back into work mode and forget everything else. 'I can recommend the chef's lunchtime specials. The Penne Arrabiata and the cannelloni.'

'Is that so?' He looked up at her with that gleam in his dark eyes again and she could feel the precious grip she had on her composure starting to slip. Probably recommending Italian dishes to an Italian wasn't her best move.

'They are very good.' She tried to angle her chin up further. She had the utmost confidence in her chef. 'Better than my Italian pronunciation of them, I assure you.'

He laughed at that. 'Actually, I didn't think your Italian pronunciation was too bad. You just need to roll your tongue around the words a little more.' He proceeded to pronounce both dishes again in a slow smooth tone that made her blood start to heat up to boiling point. How did he manage to make two ordinary dishes from a menu sound like some kind of prelude to lovemaking? she wondered distractedly. 'Well…I'll…I'll bear that in mind,' she retorted stiffly.

'Yes, you do that.' Once more there was that glimmer of amusement in his eyes and then he returned his attention to the menu.

She knew her manner was uptight, yet she couldn't seem to help it. He was having the strangest effect on her. He made her feel gauche and unsure of herself...and *he made her aware of herself as a woman*....

The knowledge trickled through her like ice.

Antonio glanced up and caught the vulnerable light in her green eyes. It was only there for a second before it was hidden behind a sweep of long dark lashes, replaced by that wary, guarded look of hers.

'So have you made up your mind?' she asked him, now fiddling nervously with the pair of glasses that sat perched on the end of her nose.

For a second he was distracted from thoughts of food as he wondered what had prompted that expression in her eyes— strange really, because he wasn't interested in her. She certainly wasn't his type.

He snapped the menu shut and handed it back to her. 'Yes, I'll go with your recommendation and have the Penne Arrabiata.'

'And to drink?' She pushed the wine list in his direction.

'Water, thanks, I need to keep a clear head for business this afternoon.'

'OK.' She started to turn away from him but he detained her. 'By the way, is your boss in today?' he asked idly.

'My boss?' She looked back at him with a frown.

'Yes. The owner of the establishment,' he enunciated clearly.

'You're looking at her.'

The surprise on his handsome features amused her.

'You're Victoria Heart?'

'That's right. Was there something you wanted to speak to me about?'

'No, not really.' For a second his eyes held with hers. For some reason he'd expected her to point out the woman now standing by the front reception area. 'You're younger than I expected you to be.'

'Am I?' She looked at him in puzzlement. 'I'm twenty-three. Sorry...but why are you interested?'

'Just curious.' His mobile phone rang and he took it out to answer it. 'Thanks for the lunch recommendation.' He gave her a brief smile and turned his attention to the call.

She knew she was being dismissed and she would gratefully have hurried away, except before she could move she heard him say, 'Yes, Antonio Cavelli speaking.'

Antonio Cavelli. She stood rigidly where she was. Was this *the* Antonio Cavelli who had purchased the hotel next door to her? She didn't pay much attention to gossip sheets, nor did she get much time to watch TV programmes, so she really wouldn't know him if she fell over him. But now she came to think about it she had heard that the multimillionaire was very attractive, very sought after by the opposite sex.

As she still made no attempt to move away, he covered the receiver of his phone and looked up, 'Thank you but I would like my lunch as quickly as possible.' His voice was curt.

'Yes...yes, of course.' Pulling herself together she hurried across to place his order with the kitchen.

It was quite a relief being within the warm busy hustle of the kitchen.

'Everything all ready for your meeting with the bank, Victoria?' Berni, the head chef, asked her as he put two plates down on the counter top, ready for one of the waitresses to collect.

'Yes, all the paperwork is in order.'

He nodded. 'You've been running a highly successful business here for the past few years. They can't say that you don't know what you are doing.'

'No, they can't say that.' Victoria smiled. When Berni had first come to work for her a year and a half ago he'd treated her with a kind of wary disdain. Then one day a few members of staff hadn't turned in and she'd rolled up her sleeves and worked alongside him. Since then they'd rubbed along together very well. And telling her she knew what she was doing was indeed an accolade coming from the temperamental chef.

'I'm sure it will all be fine,' he said blithely now.

The words made the tension that had been escalating inside her all morning twist. She didn't want to tell Berni that she wasn't quite as optimistic as him. His wife had just had a baby and he needed this job—but then so did all the other members of her staff. Not that the bank would care a damn about that. Neither would they care that she was a single mother of a two-year-old little boy and that she would be practically destitute if the business went under. All she was to the bank was a number on a sheet of paper.

Berni was right, her business had been very successful, and the bank had got more than their pound of flesh out of her in bank charges and interest over the years. But all they would look at now was the fact that her takings were down and her expenditure was significantly up, thanks to her new landlord—Lancier. So she had a horrible feeling that her visit to the bank today wasn't going to be pleasant. And given the present economic climate the odds were against them extending her loan.

Which meant she either sold up to Lancier or went bankrupt.

The very thought made her feel sick. She'd rather have sold to a flesh-eating monster than to the company who had deliberately tried to squeeze her out. But if the bank said no, then Lancier's offer was her only alternative.

Unless.

She moved back to the kitchen door and glanced out of the round porthole window towards Antonio Cavelli's table.

He could be her salvation.

She'd devised a whole new business plan around the fact that the Cavelli hotel was opening up next to her. The simple fact was that her premises would be an ideal access point for his hotel. She got a lot of passing trade on the busy main road, whilst his hotel was set back in secluded gardens. She'd been trying to get in touch with Antonio Cavelli for the past three months to tell him this and to run a few ideas by him—ideas that would give his customers a side access to his hotel, in return for her still being able to operate her business under the umbrella of his. They wouldn't even need to make any structural changes; there was already a connecting small patio garden off the back of her restaurant. They could just open the doors and walk through.

She'd emailed both him and the chairman of the company, Luc Cavelli, practically every week. Had even sent spreadsheets and business projection figures. But to no avail—they hadn't replied to one of her emails.

But now here he was, sitting in her restaurant about to have lunch.

Maybe it was fate. Or maybe he'd read her ideas and liked them. After all, he had enquired about the owner of the restaurant—*he had known her name.*

'Berni, take special care with the order for table thirty-three, will you?' she murmured absently as she moved to get a jug of ice water. Berni glanced over at her with a raised eyebrow.

'I take special care with all the orders,' he said gruffly.

She smiled. 'Yes, I know—it's just that this lunch might be the most important of the year.'

CHAPTER TWO

ANTONIO looked up as Victoria put the jug of water down on his table. He'd finished his phone call and was now browsing through some papers from his architect's office regarding the plans for the new boutiques that were to replace this restaurant.

'Thanks.' He acknowledged the water with a nod, and returned his attention to the papers. But after a moment he became aware that she was still standing next to him.

'Was there something else?' He looked back up at her enquiringly.

'Well, actually, yes. I was wondering if I could talk to you for a moment?'

He didn't make an immediate reply, just sat back in his chair and regarded her with that cool dark gaze of his.

It took all of her courage to continue. 'You're my new neighbour, aren't you? Antonio Cavelli, the hotel magnate?'

He inclined his head.

'I can't tell you how pleased I am to meet you. Do you mind if I sit down for a moment?' She didn't wait for him to reply but pulled out the chair opposite and sat down. OK, he terrified her to death—and she didn't want to do this—but she was desperate.

'Actually, I have been emailing you with some business propositions. I wonder if you got any of them?'

One dark eyebrow rose. 'No, I can't say I have.'

'It's just that as my restaurant is practically attached to your hotel, I thought we could do some business together.' She leaned forward and poured them both a glass of water as she spoke.

Despite everything Antonio found himself intrigued. When she talked about business he noticed there was a complete transformation in her manner. Her green eyes were bright with enthusiasm, her body relaxed. And she was very eloquent. It seemed she had identified the fact that a side entrance to his hotel would be of benefit to him, and had put together some kind of proposal to incorporate her restaurant within his hotel. In fact, she had worked out a whole business strategy, which did sound surprisingly competent. She obviously had a good head for figures and was very bright and very astute, but it wasn't something that he would want.

As soon as she paused for breath he held up a hand.

'Ms Heart.'

She smiled expectantly. 'Call me Victoria, please.'

'Victoria. I'm sorry, but I'm not interested—'

'But you would gain by having this entrance and—'

'Even so, I'm still not interested,' he cut across her firmly. He could see the disappointment in her eyes.

'Really?' She paused. 'It's just that I thought maybe you'd got one of my emails and it was why you'd come in here today for lunch.'

'I haven't received any of your emails,' he told her honestly. 'I was inspecting work that's being carried out next door. And the only reason I came in here for lunch was that it was convenient.'

'I see.' She bit down on her lip for a moment. She had very soft lips, he noticed; in fact, she had a nicely shaped mouth. 'Well, seeing as you are here, maybe I could leave my business plan with you?' She looked over at him hopefully. 'I have it all printed out in the office. I can put it in a folder and leave it at the reception for you to take.'

He had to hand it to her, she was tenacious. 'You can leave it if you want and I'll take it. But it's a no-go as far as I'm concerned.'

'Well, you never know—you might think differently when you look at it.' She smiled at him.

The waitress brought his food and Victoria pushed her chair back from the table and got up. 'Thanks for taking the time to listen to me,' she said politely. 'I hope you enjoy your lunch.'

After her appointment at the bank, Victoria picked Nathan up from kindergarten. And then following their usual routine she pushed him through the park in his stroller.

The sun was sending dappled light onto the path through the tracery of green branches and there was a fragrant smell from the eucalyptus trees. Hard to believe that on such a beautiful September day her life was falling apart. But it was. Because the bank had said no to her and that was her last hope.

Deep down she'd known that they wouldn't extend her credit, but it was still the most dreadful disappointment. Now it seemed that everything she had worked so hard for was slipping away.

And what on earth was she going to tell her staff? They all seemed to have the utmost faith that she would sort the business out.

How had this happened? she wondered in anguish. How could she be the owner of a successful restaurant one moment and be staring bankruptcy in the face the next? The situation had crept up on her so gradually as to be almost insidious.

Nathan wriggled impatiently in his stroller. He wanted to get out and although he didn't talk much yet he was making the fact very clear.

Victoria stopped and went around to unfasten his safety harness. 'OK, honey, you can toddle for a while now,' she told him softly, and he gave her a winning smile, his dark eyes sparkling up at her full of life and mischief.

At least she had Nathan, she thought, her heart swelling with love. He was the most important thing in her life. Everything else could be worked out.

But what would become of them now? The question made fear coil inside her like a snake. Everything she had was tied up in the business.

Victoria had experienced poverty as a child, had watched her parents scrimping and scraping to get by. They'd tried to hide the problems from her but she remembered all too well the cold hard reality of it. Her father had died when she was thirteen—the family home had been lost and for a while she and her mother had lived in a small flat in an inner city suburb of London. That had been a truly terrible time and her mother had died less than a year later, leaving Victoria under the care of social services until her mother's sister in Australia had been found and she had been sent to live with her.

She'd never met her aunt Noreen until the day she'd stepped off the plane in Sydney and she had been incredibly nervous. All she had known about the woman was that she was her mother's older sister but they hadn't been close. Deep down Victoria supposed she had been hoping for a kindly aunt— someone who resembled her mum, someone who would help heal the loneliness and loss she felt. But it had been immediately apparent that Noreen was not the sentimental type and looking after a heartbroken fourteen-year-old girl was not something she had wanted at all. In fact, she'd made it very clear from the start that she had only taken her in because she'd felt obliged to. There had been no warm hug of welcome, no platitudes about how sad the situation was—just a cool handshake and a let's-get-on-with-it attitude.

Noreen had been in her late forties, single and a formidable businesswoman. She owned a small restaurant out at Bondi Beach and she put Victoria to work there almost as soon as she arrived. 'You'll have to pay your way, girl. I can't afford passengers,' she'd told her as she tossed an apron in her direction. 'You can have two evenings off during a school week, the rest of the time you start work at six-thirty.'

Those years had been hard and the hours unsocial but Victoria had done as she was told, and had in fact shown a natural aptitude for cooking as well as for business. And Noreen had been pleased. An emotionally cold woman, she had no time for the fripperies of being a female but she had taught her well in the ways of business, encouraging her to go on to college to get business qualifications and qualifications in catering.

When she was twenty, Victoria was running Noreen's business for her single-handedly. But the hours were long and hard and she had little time for herself. And it was at this point that she had met Lee. He was a highly respected member of the business community and ten years her senior.

Looking back now she realized how naive she had been to fall for his smooth lines. But she had been very lonely and he had made her feel special—had looked at her and admired her and showed interest in her, and she had lapped it up.

But it had been a big mistake. As soon as she had gone to bed with Lee he had stopped being interested and had cut her dead and moved on to his next conquest.

She felt a wave of shame now as she remembered going to him to tell him she was pregnant, remembered the way he had calmly told her to have an abortion and had written a cheque and slid it across the desk to her.

Victoria hadn't wanted to cash that cheque; she'd wanted to tear it up and fling it in his face. She'd had no intention of having the abortion. Neither had she had any intention of allowing Noreen the pleasure of throwing her out, which her aunt had coldly insisted she would do if she went ahead with the pregnancy. Instead she'd taken a leap of faith and had used the money as a down payment for rent on a small bedsit.

'What the hell are you playing at?' Noreen had demanded as she had watched her pack a suitcase to leave.

'I'm doing what you told me I should do. I'm standing on my own two feet.'

She remembered her aunt's rage. 'You're just like your mother! Well, don't think you can come back here when the going gets tough because you can't. I'll want nothing to do with you.'

'That's OK. I won't be coming back. And just for the record my mother may have been pregnant with me when she married my dad but they were very much in love. But you wouldn't understand feelings like that.'

'Oh, I understand all right. I understand that your mother stole the only man I ever cared about, trapped him when she fell pregnant with you....'

The bitter words spilling out into the silence had explained so much about Noreen's cold, derogatory manner over the years—her almost vehement disdain for Victoria at times, the veiled insults.

She'd never seen Noreen again. Two months later on her twenty-first birthday Victoria had received a solicitor's letter. It seemed her mother had taken out a life insurance policy that had paid out on her death and the money had been invested and held in trust for Victoria.

She'd broken down and cried on the morning that letter had come. It had been a precious last gift from her mother at a point when she had needed it most, and she had made a conscious decision that she would use it to make a better life for her and her child.

And she'd done that. She'd known if she just banked the money and used it to pay rent that it would be gone in no time, that she needed to make it work for her, so she had decided to start her own business. She'd found a little bijou café to rent and had started out just selling teas and coffees and her homemade cakes. By the time Nathan was born she had been able to afford to take on another girl to help her. Six months after that she had extended her premises, and with the help of a bank loan had turned the business into a thriving restaurant with a small studio apartment attached for her and Nathan.

She'd sent Noreen a letter at that point telling her she was doing well and had even sent some photographs of Nathan, but her aunt had never acknowledged them and had never visited. Probably frightened in case she was asked for help.

She would never be that desperate, Victoria promised herself fiercely. She was a survivor—she would find a way around her problems. After all, she'd got them this far. And no matter how broke she was she would always find a way to provide for Nathan, to care for him and love him.

Nathan wanted to push his pram himself and she allowed him to take it over, smiling to herself as she watched the toddler's unsteady yet resolute progress. He'd only just turned two. But he was filled with a stubborn sense of purpose that reminded her a lot of herself.

Her phone rang and she fished it out from her pocket with a feeling of hope. Maybe it would be Antonio Cavelli— maybe he'd read her business proposition and had second thoughts about it.

'Ms Heart, this is Tom Roberts calling you from Lancier Enterprises. Just reminding you of our appointment today at four-thirty.'

Of course it wasn't Antonio Cavelli; he'd told her he wasn't interested in her proposal. Victoria swallowed on a hard painful knot in her throat. But she wasn't ready to admit defeat and sign away her precious business yet, she told herself fiercely. *Especially to Lancier!* 'Ah, yes, Mr Roberts. I rang and left a message with your secretary earlier today, stating that I was unable to make our appointment. Unfortunately I've no child care for my little boy. Could we reschedule for later in the week?'

'Later in the week doesn't suit, Ms Heart.' The man's tone was furious. 'May I suggest you bring your child with you into the office. We need to discuss terms today. Otherwise I can't promise that this generous offer for your business will be on the table tomorrow.'

'How's it going?' Antonio's lazy question coming from the doorway made the accountant jump nervously as he put the phone down. He hadn't noticed his boss standing there.

'Everything's in hand.' The words were firmly decisive, but Tom Roberts looked anything but in control of the situation. In fact, he looked completely flustered.

'I take it Ms Heart is still trying to give you the runaround?' Antonio moved further into the office.

'She's trying to be a little elusive but it's nothing I can't handle.'

'Hmm.' For a second Antonio remembered the way Victoria Heart had approached him with her business idea this afternoon, fixing him with those wide green intelligent eyes.

Why he was thinking about that he didn't know. He really had more important matters on his mind right now. He sauntered over to the fax machine by the side of Tom's desk and took out the documents his lawyer had sent for him.

The sooner he relieved his father of his shares in the company, the better, he thought angrily as he scanned the details of his directive. The old man had obviously lost his sanity completely—either that or he was having some kind of laugh at his expense!

This pretence that he was giving him an ultimatum because he cared about him and wanted him to settle down instead of working so hard was frankly ludicrous! The only thing that Luc Cavelli had ever cared about was himself. And he'd always had an over-inflated sense of his own importance, an arrogance that seemed to have spilled now into some kind of obsession with Antonio providing him with the future generation of the Cavelli family.

Please!

Antonio shook his head. He'd told his father once that he had no intention of ever marrying; and he'd meant it. He knew his limitations and he knew he wasn't the settling-down type. He enjoyed his freedom too much, enjoyed playing the field. In that respect he was probably like his father—but unlike his father he thought about the consequences of his actions, and he believed in being honest with himself and with the women he dated. The mess of his parents' marriage had been a stark warning against anything else.

As for bringing some poor unsuspecting child into the world just to gain some shares in a business, or to fulfil his father's ambitions! Well, the man could think again. A child was the biggest commitment of all and definitely off Antonio's agenda.

The old guy really had lost it if he thought for one moment he would do something so irresponsible!

But if the old guy had lost it—*really lost it*—what would that mean for the future of the company? The thought occurred to Antonio that whilst he could walk away back to his other company unscathed, there were thousands—literally thousands—of jobs on the line at Cavelli.

'Anyway, I laid the law down to her,' Tom Roberts was saying smugly. 'Told her the deal wouldn't be on the table tomorrow if she didn't get herself down here.'

Antonio was barely listening. He had his back to the guy and was reading the directive from his father and the attached documentation.

I'm not getting any younger, Antonio. All I ask is that you marry and provide me with a grandchild. Once you have done that I will happily hand over all of my shares in the business to you.

'Anyway, she came to heel pretty quickly. She knows we've made a damn good offer.'

Tom's voice was like an annoying drone. 'Great...' Antonio murmured distractedly. He looked up from the papers in his hand and out of the window at the street below.

There was a taxi pulling up at the curb, and as Antonio watched he saw Victoria Heart step out onto the pavement.

It looked as if Tom was right. Well, that was one less problem to sort out, he told himself wryly. He was about to turn away when he noticed that she had a child in her arms and that she was struggling to get a pushchair out from the back seat.

He frowned. 'I didn't know that Ms Heart had a child.'

'Yes, she's a single mother. I did some digging when I was researching her. She's never been married and there's no man on the scene and no maintenance for the child.' Tom's voice was derisive. 'Another reason why she can't afford to turn us down.'

Antonio stilled.

'Anyway, leave it with me,' the man told him briskly. 'I'll have the deal signed and sealed for you within the next hour.'

'I've changed my mind....'

'Sorry?' Tom looked over at him in surprise.

'I've changed my mind. Tell Victoria Heart when she arrives that this deal is off and then get my secretary to show her through to my office.'

'But...' Tom turned an interesting shade of beetroot. 'But...'

With a smile Antonio returned to his office. He'd found the perfect solution to the problem his father had posed. And that solution was Victoria Heart.

'What do you mean the deal's off?' Victoria looked at the accountant in horror, all colour draining from her face. She'd thought that the worst thing that could possibly happen was selling her business to Lancier but now she knew differently. The worst thing was if this sale fell through, because it meant bankruptcy for certain.

'My boss has changed his mind.' Tom shrugged. 'I told you not to delay—I warned you.'

Victoria transferred Nathan over to her other arm as the child wriggled to get down. She was trying very hard to keep calm, but as she stood watching the man coolly shuffling papers on his desk, the feeling was getting further and further away. 'But we only spoke a few moments ago on the phone!'

'As I said, it's nothing to do with me now.' Tom shrugged again. 'Take it up with the owner of the company. He said you could go through and see him.' He closed the files in front of him and looked up. 'It's the door at the end of the hallway. I'll get his secretary to show you through—'

Before he had finished speaking Victoria had swung out of the room and was heading down the hallway. She wasn't waiting around for any secretary; she needed this sorting out—now.

Without knocking she opened the door and strode into the large sunlit office. And for a moment she thought she had entered some kind of parallel universe as her eyes met with the man's behind the desk.

Antonio Cavelli!

What was he doing here? Her mind struggled with the situation and she stood nonplussed, holding onto the child in her arms as if he were her only lifeline to sanity.

Antonio by contrast seemed perfectly relaxed; he was lounging back in the leather chair behind his desk, talking in Italian to someone on the phone. He glanced over and motioned for her to take a seat opposite to him. 'Won't be a moment,' he told her in English before returning to his conversation.

Victoria didn't move. She was aware of the secretary from the outer office coming into the room behind her and whispering a rather breathless apology about Victoria's intrusion, but she was waved away dismissively. Then the door closed.

'As far as I can see this is the perfect solution,' Antonio told his lawyer in Italian as his gaze moved slowly over Victoria, inspecting her from the tip of her flat-heeled shoes up over the unflattering mid-calf-length skirt before lingering on her left hand to make sure she wore no ring. He smiled. 'But don't get me wrong, Roberto. This will just be a marriage on paper—a business move. I'll divorce her once the shares are mine. But what makes this so perfect is that she already has a child.' His eyes rested on the little boy in her arms as he listened to what his lawyer had to say and he noticed how protectively she held him in against her slender body.

'I've read the documents, Roberto. The old man has forgotten to stipulate that the child must be a direct bloodline to the Cavelli family. He hasn't even said anything about the Cavelli name. So you see where I'm going with this…a marriage of convenience to a woman who already has a child is perfect.' Antonio's lips curved in a triumphant smile as he imagined his father's horror when he realized his mistake and yet still had to hand over all of his shares in the business. It was the perfect revenge. In fact, Antonio could hardly wait now to tie the knot and present this woman as his wife—was looking forward to seeing the expression on his father's face when he saw her and her illegitimate child and realized he'd been outmanoeuvred, had lost control of the business.

'I'll leave it in your capable hands, Roberto—I want a watertight contract and prenuptial agreement drawing up immediately.' He leaned forward and flicked through the calendar on his desk. 'I'm due to fly home to Italy next Monday. So I could marry her that afternoo… Yes, I have a couple of hours free before the flight—that gives you over a week to do your magic with the legal side of things. I'll get all her details, child's full name, et cetera, and get back to you.'

Antonio replaced the receiver and silence fell in the office like a blanket of ice. She was glaring at him, her green eyes narrowed like a cat, wary, cornered and ready to pounce.

'Take a seat.' He spoke in English again and waved her towards the chair opposite but still she didn't move. She hadn't understood a word he'd been saying on the phone but she'd noticed the way he had looked at her and her whole body

was still tingling in consternation. He'd made her feel as if
she was some kind of object being weighed up ready for
auction and found wanting.

How dare he look at her like that! Who the hell did he
think he was?

'So what exactly is going on here?' Her voice wasn't quite
steady and she hated herself for that. She wanted to be in
control, and she certainly didn't want him to know just how
nervous he made her feel. 'I take it you're the man behind this
takeover deal for my restaurant?' She tipped her head up
proudly. 'And that you've been hiding behind another
company's name?'

'I am Lancier. I own the company.' He sounded completely at ease.

'That's as may be, but it's a fact that you conveniently
forgot to mention when you were in my restaurant today!'

'I was in your restaurant to have lunch, not discuss business.'
He sat back in his chair and regarded her steadily. 'As you know,
my accountant, Tom Roberts, has been running the Australian
side of my business. I've just flown in to look over things.'

'And you've decided you no longer want to buy the lease
on my restaurant?' Her voice was softer now—all the anger
and recriminations buried behind a far heavier weight of worry.

'I've had second thoughts about the situation…yes.'
Antonio was distracted slightly as the child in her arms turned
to regard him with steady dark eyes.

'Do you mind telling me why?' She whispered the question
numbly as she transferred her son to her other hip.

For a moment the shapeless jacket was twisted to one side,
revealing a glimpse of what appeared to be a very shapely body.

Antonio felt a dart of surprise and his eyes drifted over her
more slowly, deliberately assessing her again—but the jacket
was back in place now and it was hard to tell what her body
was like under its baggy shape.

Realizing what he was doing, he stopped suddenly. This was about business, he reminded himself angrily, nothing else.

'I was getting around to my reasons.' He nodded towards the chair. 'Sit down, Victoria.'

Their eyes clashed and he realized she had noticed his momentary interest and that she was blushing. He cursed himself.

'Sit down, Victoria,' he said again, and this time his tone was even more briskly businesslike.

Victoria did as she was told, her legs shaking. Had she just imagined that second bold assessment of her body? Her eyes met with his and the flame of heat inside her intensified.

How mortifying! She knew damn well that Antonio Cavelli was not remotely interested in her—that he was so arrogantly sure of himself that he probably looked at every woman in the same way. Yet here she was, blushing like a school girl! She needed to get a grip!

'Have you read my business plan?' she asked suddenly, angling her chin upwards again and meeting his gaze.

She was still blushing. Antonio found it quite amusing. He was used to sophisticated women of the world and her reaction to him intrigued him.

His gaze drifted over her face. And he found himself wondering abstractedly what she would look like without the glasses that were still perched on her nose—they completely dominated her face and did nothing for her.

'Business plan?' For a second he couldn't remember what she was talking about. Then he remembered the folder her receptionist had handed to him earlier today. 'Oh, that—no. I thought I made it clear this morning. Your idea isn't something I would consider.'

'But—'

'Victoria, I have a plan that could bail you out with the restaurant but I'm on limited time here. I have an important meeting in twenty minutes so if we could press on.' He leaned forward impatiently and she shrank back into her chair.

There was an aura of power about him that unnerved her completely, or was it that raw sensuality that seemed to blaze from his dark eyes? He was everything a man should be and more. The clothes he wore were expensive and sophisticated, his features chiselled in a ruggedly handsome way, the square jaw accentuating his masculinity. He made her achingly aware of her own femininity and inadequacies.

'Tell me, are you married?' he asked abruptly.

'Married?' The question took her completely aback. She shook her head in confusion. 'No, why are you asking me that?'

'And you live alone? There's no man in your life?' he pressed on.

'That's…really none of your business!' she stammered. 'What's all this about?'

'I'll take that as a no, shall I?' He brushed aside her question and then held up a hand as she started to interrupt him. 'You're right, it's none of my business.' He conceded the point easily. 'The thing is, I have a proposition for you.'

She could feel her heart thudding unevenly against her chest. 'What kind of a proposition?'

He caught the nervous look in her wide eyes and his lips twitched with amusement. 'A strictly business proposition, I assure you.'

The dry note in his voice made her skin start to heat with embarrassed colour again. But she managed to hold his gaze defiantly. OK, he was making it clear that he wasn't interested in her sexually—but she wasn't interested in him either. All she cared about was her business. 'Good, so perhaps you'd better make yourself clearer. Do you want to buy the lease on my restaurant or not?'

'To be perfectly honest, I've never wanted to buy your restaurant. What I wanted was for you to vacate the premises. I have redevelopment plans for that area.'

The blunt reply wasn't at all what she had expected. 'You mean you want to knock the place down…?'

'Pretty much…yes, but I'm prepared to be very generous to you, Victoria,' he cut across her smartly, one eye on his watch. He couldn't waste much more time on this. 'What I'm proposing now is that I relocate your business to a position of your choice within the city. I will bear all costs including staff's wages for the transitional period, fittings and fixtures for your new premises, plus advertising costs, and I will handsomely compensate you for the inconvenience. Shall we say double the amount of money we offered you in the first instance?'

Her eyes widened. 'So what's the catch?' her voice was huskily unsure. 'Why are you suddenly prepared to pay so much?'

'Because I want something from you in return.'

Nathan was wriggling on her knee. He was bored and wanted to get down, but she held him where he was safely wrapped in her arms. 'You mean apart from my allowing you to bulldoze my lovely restaurant?'

'I think I've covered that with a more than generous offer,' Antonio replied easily. 'You'll be financially made for life if I back you in your new venture. No, what I want from you is a little piece of your time.'

Her eyes narrowed on him suspiciously.

'I'm in need of a wife.'

The statement was made so nonchalantly that at first Victoria wondered if she had heard him correctly. 'Sorry, did you say…a wife?'

He smiled. 'Don't look so worried, this is a marriage for business purposes only. I don't want you in my bed—and there will be nothing improper about the arrangement.'

Victoria shook her head and tried to gather her senses up from the fragmented emotions whirling inside of her. She knew full well that Antonio Cavelli was the type of man who could have any woman he pleased, and that she wouldn't be on his list of most desirable females. 'So…run this by me again. Why exactly do you need a wife? And why are you asking me to do this?'

'I'm asking you because you're convenient. I'm in need of a ready-made family for a short-term period without any strings or complications. You will do nicely.' He reached for the calendar on his desk. 'It's a case of being in the right place at the right time,' he added with a smile as he flicked through the pages.

'Lucky me, then.' Her voice was low and tight as she fought to suppress the anger rising inside of her. 'But perhaps you'd care to explain in a little more detail exactly what these business reasons are.'

'You don't need to worry about details, Victoria.' He reached for a pen on the desk. 'It's complicated and to do with a transfer of shares within my company. Nothing for you to concern yourself with.'

The patronizing tone made her head snap up and her eyes blaze into his. 'Too complicated for someone like me…is that what you are trying to say?'

'No, that's not what I'm trying to say.' He stopped what he was doing and looked at her. 'You're obviously an intelligent woman so let me rephrase that for you—*it's none of your business.*'

There was a steely strength behind the words that let her know in no uncertain terms that he was the one calling the shots—and that he was only doing her a favour humouring her questions to a point.

She swallowed nervously but forced herself to continue. 'I have a child to think about, Mr Cavelli—a child whose welfare comes first above everything else in my life. And I think as you are asking me to marry you I have a right to know exactly what is going on?'

He frowned. 'I thought I made myself clear—this isn't a real proposal. I am not interested in you or your child on a personal level—this is just business.'

'Yes, you've made that point.' Victoria's cheeks started to turn a bright rosy red. 'But I still need more information—'

'The only information you need is that the arrangement is perfectly above board and that I will treat you and your son with the greatest care and respect for the time you are under my roof and legally my obligation.'

'Under your roof…' Victoria started to shake her head. The thought of spending time in the same house as this man made her senses fly into panic. 'No…I don't think so. It's one thing putting my name on a piece of paper for you and quite another moving in with you.'

Antonio looked vaguely amused. There were women queuing around the block who were desperate to move in with him…women who would marry him in an instant with just the snap of his fingers. And yet this…plain woman was looking at him as if he were an ogre from the blue lagoon. Amazing!

However, it made her even more perfect for his requirements, he thought as he transferred his attention to the calendar again. He would never ask one of the women waiting in the wings to do this. It would be too fraught with emotional complications, and that was something he was determined to avoid at all costs.

'Don't worry, I'll probably only want you for about…let's see…' Antonio paused to calculate how long it would take to transfer his father's shares into his name. The old man would probably kick up a hell of a fuss but as everything was in writing… 'Say about a month—give or take a few weeks,' he finished resolutely. 'As soon as my business transaction is completed we can have the marriage dissolved and go our separate ways—no need to see each other ever again.'

The cool words whirled around like a cyclone inside of her. 'You don't have much respect for the institution of marriage, do you, Mr Cavelli?'

'As I said before, this is business.' Antonio looked over at her with a raised eyebrow. 'But if the deal isn't for you, then I'll get someone else.'

Victoria nodded in relief. She really wasn't comfortable with any of this. 'I think that might be best.'

Antonio frowned and leaned back in his chair. He really hadn't anticipated that! Most people would have snatched his hand off for this kind of money! 'Best for whom—certainly not your son?' His eyes drifted to the child on her knee. The little boy was playing with a button on her jacket, a look of absorbed concentration on his young face. Antonio couldn't help noticing that the material of the jacket was rather worn, whilst the child's clothes seemed new by comparison. 'You do realize that this will make all the difference to his life, don't you? It will mean private education and a nice home. And what's your alternative? I've looked at your accounts, Victoria, and even by the most optimistic of calculations you only have two to three weeks left before your business folds and the bailiffs turn up at your door.'

She'd been in the process of gathering the child up and getting to her feet but she sank back down again now. 'You mean the deal is off completely?'

'What did you expect?' He spread his hands.

'I thought…I thought you might go back to your original offer for the place?'

Antonio made no reply, just shook his head and there was a steely expression on the handsome features now.

'But you need me out of those premises, Mr Cavelli, you said so yourself.'

'I can wait.' His eyes held with hers calmly.

Desperately she tried to swallow down the panic that was rising inside of her again. 'Well, I'm not going anywhere without a fight.' From somewhere she found the strength to hold her ground.

Antonio couldn't help admiring her spirit. But he really didn't have the time or the inclination to be philanthropic and allow her to walk away. He wanted this deal wrapped up before his father got wind of his mistake and started to back-track. Besides, this deal would benefit her in the long run.

'Hard to fight without money, and believe me, Victoria, you don't want to lock horns with me because you will be crushed.'

The hard cold words hit her like a punch.

In that moment she hated him—hated his arrogance and his confidence and his power. And more than anything hated the fact that he was right. She could bluster all she wanted but there was no way she could win a fight against this multimillionaire tycoon.

He noted the vulnerable look flickering over her young face and knew with the experience born from many a successful business deal that it was now time to reel her in. 'Anyway, your loss. I'll get my secretary to show you out.'

'No!' She stopped him before he could reach for the phone and he smiled at her, a light of triumph in the darkness of his eyes now.

'I thought you'd see sense.' He lifted his pen and put a red *X* on the calendar. 'I have two hours free next Monday afternoon. We'll sign the paperwork at two…get married at two-thirty.'

Victoria said nothing. The marriage wasn't going to happen, she reassured herself fiercely. She was just agreeing with him to buy herself time. By next week she'd have found a way out of this. There had to be a way out—*there just had to be*.

CHAPTER THREE

'THAT gorgeous guy is here again in the restaurant.'

Emma put her head around the door of Victoria's apartment, a look of excitement on her young face. 'And he says he wants to see you.'

Victoria didn't need to ask her receptionist which guy she meant—she knew full well there was only one man who could cause such a flurry of excitement and she felt an immediate thrust of nervous anticipation.

It had been two days since she had seen Antonio. Two days and two sleepless nights since she had sat in his office and played for time by agreeing to his demand to become his wife.

Since then she'd been going over and over her accounts, looking for a means of escape. She was still sorting through the paperwork now, desperately searching for some solution. But so far she had found nothing and she was starting to feel more and more hemmed in by the stark option that had been presented to her. She either married Antonio Cavelli or she lost everything that she had ever worked for.

Icy cold panic swept through her at the thought. She wasn't giving up without a fight, she told herself fiercely. Her glance moved from her receptionist back to the paperwork on her desk.

But what could she do?

'He's not here on his own,' the receptionist continued.

'He's got two other men with him and a woman. They are going to have coffee in the lounge area.'

Maybe Antonio had changed his mind, she thought suddenly. Maybe he was here to see to other business. The idea made her feel much better.

'Let me have a look.' Victoria stood and went through to the hallway that linked her apartment with the restaurant. There was a small window in the doorway behind the reception desk and if she stood on tiptoe she could see Antonio Cavelli standing nonchalantly chatting with some other people.

When she'd lain awake in the darkness of the night there had been a part of her that had wondered if she had imagined how attractive he was, how powerful he was. She'd even wondered if maybe she'd mistaken his ultimatum—got the wrong end of the stick. This couldn't be happening for real, could it?

But now, looking at him, she realized she hadn't imagined anything. He was every inch the forceful, dynamic business-man in his expensive suit, his dark hair gleaming under the subdued lighting. The type of man who always got what he wanted. And, more worrying, even from this distance he seemed to exude a magnetising attractiveness that made her senses go into hyperdrive.

Frankly he scared her to death. She dragged her gaze away from him to scan the people who accompanied him—one she recognised as the accountant, Tom Roberts; the second was a man in his late thirties who was also wearing a smart suit and wasn't bad looking but nowhere in the league of Antonio Cavelli. The third was a woman in her early twenties. She was very attractive—probably just Antonio's type—long straight blonde hair and a figure to die for encased in a tight black pencil skirt and short cropped jacket.

Victoria looked away from her and back towards Antonio and as she did he glanced towards the doorway and their eyes met through the glass. The shock was intense and she stepped away from the window as if she'd been shot.

Maybe he hadn't really seen her, she told herself calmly. And even if he had—so what!

'You OK, Victoria?' Emma asked from behind her.

'Yes, of course.' She tried to smile. But she wasn't OK; she was anything but OK. Her heart was racing; she felt completely panic-stricken.

'Shall I tell him you'll be out in a minute?'

The question made Victoria glance down at her attire. She hadn't planned to work in the restaurant this morning so she was just wearing an old pair of black trousers and a plain white T-shirt. She couldn't go out there looking like this! But then she didn't possess anything much better to change into. She hadn't bought herself any new clothes for more than a year—hadn't taken any wages out of the business, hadn't done anything for herself. Any spare cash went towards getting Nathan all that he needed and keeping this restaurant up and running. And by the time she had paid her staff and Nathan's nursery fees there was nothing left.

'Tell him…tell him I'm busy doing office work and could we…reschedule…' As she spoke she saw Emma's eyebrows starting to rise.

'Do I have to tell him that?' Emma asked warily. 'Somehow I don't think he's the kind of man you ask to reschedule!'

She was absolutely right, of course. Victoria bit down on her lip and moved back through to her apartment. She wanted to lock the doors and pull down all the blinds on her windows—that or run as far away from here as her shaking legs would carry her. There were times when it was brilliantly convenient having her living accommodation in with her work, but today was definitely not one of those days. 'Tell him…' The words froze on her lips. Antonio Cavelli was standing behind Emma in the doorway.

'If you have something to tell me, Victoria, you can say it to my face.'

But Victoria didn't say anything; she couldn't, because she couldn't find her voice.

Emma whirled around. 'Oh, sorry, I was just on my way back to see you now.'

'That's OK.' He smiled at the receptionist. 'You can leave us now.'

Without even a glance in Victoria's direction Emma hurried to do as he asked and closed the door behind her.

Hold on a moment, Victoria thought distractedly. This was her restaurant, her premises. Since when had her staff started taking orders from Antonio Cavelli! How was it he suddenly seemed to be taking over her life?

'Is there a problem, Victoria?' Antonio asked her calmly.

With supreme difficulty she pulled herself together. 'The only problem is…*you*.' She didn't know where she got the strength to say that but she did, and she also managed to meet his cool dark eyes with defiance. 'These are my private quarters. You have no right to barge in here like this!'

'You should have come out into the restaurant quicker, then.' He smiled. There was something quite endearing about the way she tried to face up to him—scared rigid, yet determined to fight. 'Relax, Victoria. I've only called because we have business to sort out before the wedding next week.'

'So…you still want to go through with that?' Her voice suddenly sounded like a raw croak.

'Of course, it's all set.' His eyes moved abstractedly over her appearance as he spoke. She wasn't wearing any make-up and as usual her large glasses covered her face. Her hair was scraped back from her face in a way that did her no favours and just emphasized her pallor. As for her figure—that was hidden beneath clothes that were completely shapeless. The T-shirt looked a size too big for her, and the trousers were loose too. However, from what he could discern she did appear to have some pleasing curves hidden away under all that material, so he hadn't been completely mistaken in his observations the other day. But why on earth did she dress like that?

The blatant assessment of her clothes and her body made scalding heat flood through her. How dare he zone in on her like that! Hurriedly Victoria snatched up a cardigan from the chair beside her and put it on, wrapping the volume of grey woolly fabric around her like a shield.

'What on earth are you doing?' he asked with some amusement.

'I'm…making myself more comfortable.' She glared at him, hoping he didn't know how those bold masculine eyes of his had just turned her to jelly.

One dark eyebrow lifted sardonically.

Yes, he probably did know—just as she knew that his assessment of her was doubtless purely critical. She tried to look confident and unfazed but she was blushing uncontrollably now.

'You do realize it's about thirty degrees in here, don't you?' His glance swept away from her and around the apartment.

How on earth did she live in here? he wondered. It seemed to consist of just two rooms, which were neat and clean but incredibly basic. 'Haven't you got any air conditioning?'

The fact that he was now turning his critical attention to her home made her temperature rise even further.

'Actually I have! But I haven't switched it on today because I'm cold!' In truth she hadn't turned on the air-conditioning unit because she couldn't afford to run it and she was trying to save money whilst Nathan was out at kindergarten. But pride made her lie.

'Then you must be coming down with something,' He located the control switch for the unit and strolled across to flick it on. And immediately cool air flowed into the room.

How dared he do that! she thought angrily. Who the hell did he think he was? 'You're right, I probably *am* coming down with *something*,' she grated angrily. *'I think it's called a terminal case of cold feet, at the thought of having to marry you next week!'*

He looked over at her and amusement flickered in the darkness of his eyes. He liked her fiery sense of humour.

'Don't worry about the ceremony—it will only take ten minutes.'

The nonchalant tone annoyed her even more. 'I'm not worried about the ceremony! It's the subsequent consequences of it that are concerning me!'

Wasn't he in the least bit bothered about the enormity of what he was asking her to do?

'I assure you the only consequences will be a healthier bank account and a better way of life for you and your son.'

Obviously not in the slightest bit concerned. 'Money isn't everything, you know,' she muttered impulsively.

No one had ever said that to him before. One dark eyebrow rose and he smiled. 'You're right, of course. But it helps,' he said. He glanced around the apartment again and reluctantly she found herself seeing it through his eyes, noticing how small and utilitarian it was.

'And you need the help,' he continued coolly. 'You couldn't live here for much longer anyway. For one thing you have a growing boy. He will need space to run and play.'

'Nathan is only two years of age. I've plenty of time to think about that. In the meantime I'm bringing him up with love—and that's all that really counts.' She tipped her head up proudly, refusing to allow him to talk down to her.

'Admirable, I'm sure. But love won't pay the bills, will it?'

'We were doing OK!'

He watched how her hands clenched and unclenched at her sides. 'No, you weren't, Victoria. You were close to bankruptcy.'

'I admit trade has been slow.' Her voice was husky as she confessed that reality. 'But we would have got through! And a lot of my problems have been exacerbated by you ruthlessly hiking up my rent.'

Antonio just shook his head and glanced at his watch. 'It's called business—don't take it personally. We'll just have to make sure you don't have any overheads like that at your new premises.'

The patronizing tone made her teeth start to grind with agitation. But before she could make any retort he was sweeping on. 'So, as I was saying, this deal is very much to your advantage. And don't worry about the ceremony itself, it's just a formality. Turn up in jeans if you want—I don't care.'

'I might just do that,' she muttered. 'Then again I might not turn up at all… You never know—I might have second thoughts.' She flashed him a fulminating glare. He was so damn superior and confident. Why should he just take it for granted that she would go through with this? Why should she be the only one totally stressed out by the thought of this marriage whilst he seemed so aloof from it all!

But far from looking anxious, Antonio just met her gaze steadily. 'You're an intelligent woman—I'm sure you'll manage to turn up.'

In other words, she crossed him at her own peril. A shiver raced through her at the cool reminder and she realized she had been totally fooling herself to think that there was going to be any way out of this.

'So tell me, is your passport in order?' he demanded suddenly.

'My…passport?' Her eyes narrowed on him. 'Yes—'

'And how about the child's?'

'Nathan…' She looked at him in puzzlement. 'Well, yes…why?'

'Because we fly to Italy straight after the service.'

'Italy?' She stared at him nonplussed and she could hear her heart drumming so loudly it sounded as if it was inside her head. 'What on earth are you talking about? I'm not flying anywhere! Why would I do that, when I have a business to run here?'

'Because you're marrying me, remember?' The glint of tolerant amusement was back in his gaze now.

'But…but you didn't say anything about going to Italy!'

He watched the way she took a step backwards as if afraid he might pick her up and throw her bodily over his shoulder to carry her away. 'Victoria, I made it perfectly clear that living under my roof for the next few weeks was part of the deal.'

'But I thought you meant you had a roof here in Sydney!'

'Well, I have a few roofs in Sydney but none that I would call home. My home is on Lake Garda, and that is where we are going.'

'But you didn't tell me that!' Panic was welling up inside of her.

'Well, I'm telling you now,' he replied calmly. 'I need you in Italy.'

'I don't understand. If we are only to remain married for a few weeks why does it matter where we are—'

'Because Italy is where I live,' he repeated himself patiently. 'It will be convenient for me. Also I want to present you to my father.' His eyes swept over her again. He wondered what his father would say when he brought her into the family home. He knew very well that his father would expect him to choose some model-type socialite for a wife, someone like Antonio's last girl-friend, who had been a member of the aristocracy. Now there was the woman his father had really wanted him to marry. The thought of having her as a daughter-in-law had appealed to Luc, and he had dropped many a heavy hint about how suitable she was, how worthy of the Cavelli name. Amazing how that seemed so important to him now, yet years ago he hadn't cared one jot about how he pulled the family name into disrepute.

Antonio smiled to himself. Well, he was going to give the hypocrite something to think about. Luc would be taken aback when he saw Victoria, but he would be absolutely furious when he realized he'd been completely outmanoeuvred. And served him right, Antonio thought grimly. It would indeed be the ultimate revenge for the contempt and humiliation he had heaped upon his mother all those years ago.

'But what about my business?' Victoria asked now. 'I can't just leave it for weeks on end!'

'You can. I will make all of that possible.' Antonio swept across the objection firmly. 'You are coming to Italy with me—it's non-negotiable.'

'For how long?'

'I told you, for a few weeks—a couple of months at the most.'

'And then we get our divorce?'

'Yes.' He glanced at his watch. 'Now, let's move on, shall we? I have a busy day ahead of me.'

Victoria stared at him helplessly. She was sure there were other questions she needed to ask him. But she couldn't think straight. This was all moving far too quickly for her.

'We'll bring the team through here,' he continued. 'It would probably be better than out in the restaurant anyway. It's more private here.'

'The team…?'

'The people who are going to project manage your restaurant for you.'

'I can manage my own restaurant!'

'You're playing in a different league now, Victoria.'

His tone reminded her of someone who was indulging a belligerent child and as he spoke he went to the door and beckoned her receptionist. 'Tell my colleagues that they can come through please.'

Victoria watched as 'the team' filtered in through her door. In the restaurant their smart businesslike appearance hadn't looked out of place, but in her tiny studio with its basic decor and furnishings they looked like aliens visiting a new planet.

'We'll use the coffee table.' Antonio directed them over towards the sofa and Victoria watched as the woman picked up Nathan's favourite teddy and moved it away from the area as if it were contaminated matter.

Awkwardly Victoria reached to take it from her and the

woman smiled coolly. 'Congratulations on your forthcoming marriage.'

'Thanks.' Victoria didn't know what else to say. She was surprised that anyone even knew about the wedding because Antonio had impressed upon her the need for secrecy when she had left his office last week. She darted a glance nervously over at him.

'It's OK—everyone in this room can be trusted to keep our secret.'

Did that mean they all knew it was just a marriage of convenience? she wondered.

She placed Nathan's teddy back in the box of toys by the doorway and then stood awkwardly, watching the people who were now spreading files and books out on her table. She didn't want them here—she wanted her life back.

'Allow me to introduce you,' Antonio continued. 'Claire is in charge of relocating you, and putting together the design and layout for your new restaurant. Harry is one of my top chefs and he is going to oversee the day-to-day running of the restaurant while you are away. And Tom of course you already know—he will be overseeing expenditure.'

As Victoria's gaze lighted on the familiar accountant he gave her a rather dour nod of acknowledgement. He obviously wasn't happy with this arrangement.

Well, that makes two of us, Victoria thought.

'Look, I appreciate that you are all just following orders and trying to do your jobs.' She spoke briskly to the group before they could put any more files out onto her table. 'But ultimately I would like to be the one who is making the decisions about my own restaurant—'

Everyone stopped and looked over at Antonio.

He shook his head and motioned for them to continue, which they did immediately. 'You are in control here, Victoria. The team are answerable to you and are only here to help you.'

Who was he kidding? Victoria thought. These people were

here to do his bidding. But she said nothing—what was the point when she was so helplessly outmanoeuvred?

'I've selected a few premises for you to look at,' Claire was saying as she opened up one of the files. 'This one is situated on Darling Harbour…and this one is in the Rocks area…'

Victoria's eyes widened as the woman slid the books across for her. The addresses were all in prime locations, and judging by the specifications on the first few pages they all looked to be freehold and, under ordinary circumstances, well out of her reach financially. Slowly she flicked through the glossy photographs.

'As per my remit I've selected premises that come with self-contained apartments,' Claire continued. 'This one also has an outside dining area for guests, plus a small private garden and swimming pool.' She turned over the pages to show Victoria the one she was referring to.

The place was stunning! 'That will cost a fortune!' she murmured.

Tom Roberts muttered something under his breath that Victoria couldn't catch but sounded a bit like, *Too right.*

'If you want it, Victoria, you only have to say the word and it's yours,' Antonio said smoothly.

She glanced over and met his steady gaze. She really couldn't weigh this situation up, couldn't weigh him up. One moment he seemed the most hateful of people and the next the most generous.

'So do you like the one with the garden and swimming pool?' Claire asked.

'Of course she likes it!' Tom interjected irately.

'Tom!' Antonio's voice was deathly quiet yet held a warning note that made the man turn a shade paler and clam up immediately.

'I do like it…' Victoria acknowledged cautiously as she glanced down and read over the details. 'But of course I will have to go and look at it.'

'That's not a problem. I'll organize viewings for you this afternoon,' Claire said immediately.

'Well, I'll leave you to go over the details,' Antonio said as he glanced at his watch. 'I have a meeting with my architect.'

'You're leaving us?' Victoria looked over at him in consternation. She didn't know which was worse—having him here or being left on her own with these people!

'Afraid I must.' He smiled at her. 'But the team will attend to everything you need. And Tom will organize a line of credit for you to make sure that you are not struggling and the restaurant runs smoothly through this transition period.' Antonio glanced over at his accountant. 'You'll make sure Victoria has everything she needs, won't you, Tom?'

'Of course.' The words seemed to stick in the man's throat and Antonio smiled to himself. He hadn't liked the way Tom had dealt with Victoria over these past few months so getting him to kowtow to her now was, in his opinion, a just punishment.

'I'll leave you all to your work.' As Antonio headed purposefully towards the door Victoria followed.

'So what's the catch?' she demanded, closing the door behind her so that the people inside couldn't hear.

'Catch?' Antonio turned and looked at her with a frown.

'Come on, Antonio, you are moving me to a wonderful location and better premises, and now you are organizing a line of credit for me here…. What's the payback?'

'You know the payback.' He turned to face her and she suddenly wished she hadn't closed the door, because the narrow confinements of the corridor meant she was too close to him.

Her heart bounced unsteadily in her chest as she thought about what he was asking her to do. 'I'm to be your wife in a business arrangement…but…how much rent will you want for these new premises? How much interest will you want back on the loan you are offering?' She forced herself to meet the darkness of his gaze. 'People don't organize lines of credit without wanting steep returns.'

'I've already stated my terms Victoria. I don't want anything else.' He said the words quietly. 'There will be no rent to pay and you can look on the money as a gift.'

'A gift?'

'Yes, a gift.' For a second his eyes drifted over her, noticing the wary expression in her green catlike eyes. But then, she'd looked at him like that from the first moment he'd walked into her restaurant, he reminded himself, and that was before she'd even realized who he was…before he'd offered her this deal. She'd obviously been very hurt in the past. Probably had difficulty trusting men even under normal circumstances—*and these were anything but normal circumstances!*

He wondered what her story was, and then frowned. He didn't care what her story was. They were just passing ships. 'Look, Victoria…' He paused for a moment as he noticed how she had tried to step back from him in the small space. 'You have nothing to be frightened about…OK? Just stick to your side of the bargain.'

The sudden gentleness of his tone took her aback. 'I'm not frightened!' She looked up at him defiantly. 'I just need to know exactly what you are expecting of me.'

'I'm not expecting anything. All you have to do is turn up, become my wife, have a few months in Italy and then we'll call it a day.'

'You make it sound so uncomplicated but—'

'It will be uncomplicated, Victoria. Because that's what I want,' he cut across her firmly. 'In fact, we'll probably be able to get the marriage annulled at the end of our time together as it won't be consummated.'

In other words, not consummating the marriage would be the easiest thing in the world for him. The knowledge should have filled her with nothing but relief, and yet as she looked at him there was a raw swirling painful feeling inside of her that she didn't understand. She supposed it was hurt pride—

which was ridiculous! She knew she wasn't his type and she didn't want to be!

'Well, that's one good thing!' She tipped her head up proudly. 'You know, I don't understand why you just haven't asked one of your girlfriends or lovers to do this. Surely it would have been easier?'

'I don't think so.' His eyes held steadily with hers. 'I don't want any messy emotional entanglement, Victoria—that's the whole point. That's why you are so perfect.'

Humiliated colour flared in her cheeks. Did he have to be quite so blunt? She got the picture! She knew she wasn't nearly glamorous enough or beautiful enough for him. Knew he was a player and not remotely likely to fall for her.

She angled her chin up even higher. 'So, I'm to play the chaste little wife in Italy whilst you carry on as normal with your girlfriends? Is that the plan?'

He frowned. 'Believe it or not, I do have some respect for the institution of marriage, Victoria—and I believe in being honest. I wouldn't hurt anyone like that!'

'I wouldn't be hurt! I wouldn't care!' She flung the words at him angrily, hurt pride sizzling inside her like a cauldron dangerously close to boiling over.

'That's as may be, but I still wouldn't do it.' His voice was curiously gentle. 'And I will look after you. Believe it or not I am capable of exercising restraint in the absence of temptation.' His lips twisted wryly.

She swallowed hard. He could break a woman's heart without even realizing he was doing it, she thought suddenly.

'I can look after myself—'

He placed a finger over her lips, silencing her. It was a nonchalant light-hearted touch, but it made her skin tingle with heated reaction. 'I will take care of you. It will be OK,' he said softly. 'You have my word.'

For a second his eyes rested on the vulnerable curve of her lips, then his gaze moved to lock with hers and she felt the sharp pull of some strange emotion twisting painfully inside of her.

He released her abruptly and her stomach flipped as if she were dizzy.

'The terms of our marriage will all be put in writing for you,' he continued smoothly. 'And I'll send the contracts for you to read in advance of signing.'

How could he touch her like that and then blend the subjects of marriage and fidelity so smoothly into a business context? she wondered hazily. She swallowed on a knot of emotion that for some reason seemed to have lodged in her throat.

What the hell was wrong with her? she wondered angrily. She should be telling him in no uncertain terms that she would be scouring his contract for any anomalies because she didn't and *couldn't* trust him! But the crazy thing was her voice seemed to have deserted her.

'Oh, and one last thing,' he added. 'Don't take any nonsense from Tom—he's just the accountant. You're calling the shots with your business now.'

Did he expect her to thank him? She felt anger and confusion vying for first place inside of her.

But obviously no reply was necessary because the next moment he was heading back into the restaurant, leaving her staring after him.

She could still feel her lips tingling and she put her hand over them, willing the reaction to stop.

How could such a light touch disturb her so deeply?

Taking a deep breath she turned back towards her apartment and reminded herself fiercely that Antonio Cavelli wasn't her ally—he was her enemy. The only reason he was telling her he'd take care of her whilst generously bailing her out now was because it suited him.

She couldn't afford to lose sight of that. She had to keep all her barriers up and be wary.

Because next week, no matter how much he tried to play it down, there would be payback. Next week he was the enemy she would be obliged to marry!

CHAPTER FOUR

As Victoria was swept along in the chauffeur-driven limousine she tried not to think in too much depth about what she was doing.

Best to keep her mind a careful blank, she told herself firmly. Because the mantra that had been helping her to keep everything together over these past few days was wearing thin. The line she'd been spinning herself about being able to deal with this wedding in a businesslike, detached way was sounding more and more hollow.

She hadn't seen Antonio since the day he'd brought his team around to her apartment. But little by little he had been taking her over, letting her know from behind the scenes that he was in control now.

And the whole thing terrified her.

In fact, last night when she had brought down her old suitcase from the back of the wardrobe to pack for Italy she had felt almost sick with apprehension. She'd found herself remembering all the promises she'd made to herself on the day she left her aunt's house about being in control of her own destiny, about never allowing anyone—*man or woman*—to hurt her or use her again.

She'd been scared back then, but she'd been determined to build a future that was secure and happy for her child. And when Nathan was born and placed into her arms that need to love him and protect him and provide for him had grown ever stronger inside of her. She'd wanted him to have all the security she'd never had. And she'd tried so hard, worked so hard.

Yet failed. Here she was adrift and at the mercy of a man who…terrified her.

Victoria closed her eyes and willed herself not to think about the effect that Antonio Cavelli had on her. This marriage was just a short-term business deal, a stepping stone that would help to provide her son with the life she wanted for him.

When she signed on the dotted line this morning, and became Mrs Antonio Cavelli, not only would her finances be back in the black they would be healthier than they ever had before. She would be the owner of a new stylish business in one of the best areas in town, with no exorbitant overheads— a business that came with massive living accommodation, and a garden and swimming pool for Nathan to play in.

There would be no more scrimping and making do; she would be able to give her son the best.

And whilst they were away in Italy everything was going to be managed as per her requirements and set up ready for her return.

They were estimating that the opening day for the new restaurant would be six weeks.

One of the few moments of joy she'd experienced this week was telling her staff that they were all keeping their jobs and even getting a pay rise.

And they deserved it, because they had all worked so hard for her, had become like a family to her over the past few years, helping her through the tough times, covering shifts for her when Nathan was ill, helping keep an eye on him on evenings when she'd had to work and he was tucked safely up in his little cot in the annex room off the kitchen.

She glanced down at the little boy on her knee and kissed the top of his silky dark hair.

How could this not be the right thing? The money that Antonio had placed in her account would mean things were going to get easier from now on, she told herself fiercely. There would be no more having to lift Nathan from his slumber at midnight to carry him through to his other cot in the apartment when she'd finished a shift.

He'd never complained, always gone easily back to sleep. Her heart squeezed a little as she looked down at him.

She'd bought him a new outfit for today and he looked adorable in the white shirt and navy-blue trousers, teamed with a navy-blue waistcoat.

She loved him so much—surely anything that made his life better was the right thing.

The limousine was slowing down now and she glanced out of the window. They were nearing the registry office.

She swallowed hard. *This was just a business deal...just a means to an end,* she repeated the words fiercely. But they weren't helping. For some reason every time she pictured herself saying her wedding vows, pictured Antonio putting a ring on her finger, her heart seemed to dip somewhere down into her stomach and dissolve.

Get a grip, Victoria, she told herself angrily.

The limousine pulled to a halt at the curb and the chauffeur got out to open the car door for her. She was aware as she stepped into the sunshine that a few passers-by turned to look over at her—probably expecting a traditionally radiant, beautiful bride in a white dress, she thought. Well, they were out of luck today. There was nothing traditional about this wedding.

She hadn't even bought herself anything new to wear.

Antonio's comment about not caring how she looked had stopped her from even trying to make a special effort. Why should she care if he didn't? And anyway, she didn't feel comfortable spending his money on her clothes—had decided that the money he'd advanced would only be used for either the business or Nathan.

So she was just wearing a plain navy-blue suit and white blouse that she wore for work sometimes. And it was perfectly adequate, she reassured herself, because as he'd pointed out quite succinctly, this *was* just business.

Holding Nathan tightly in her arms she thanked the driver and then slowly made her way inside.

She passed a young couple, obviously just married and very much in love, a group of friends surrounding them waiting to throw confetti. Their joyful laughter seemed to echo down the hallway as she stepped past them.

She'd told no one about her wedding. Her friends and colleagues had drawn their own conclusions when she'd told them she was going away for a few weeks. Most of them thought she was just going with Nathan on a well-deserved holiday. Emma, her receptionist, had taken it one step further and assumed she had a man in her life!

'About time you indulged in a bit of romance and happiness,' she'd said solemnly when Victoria had taken her leave of the restaurant earlier. 'You spend far too much time working. Go and enjoy…make mad passionate love to this guy, whoever he is…'

The memory swirled uncomfortably now with the laughter from outside.

She didn't know what on earth had put such an idea in Emma's head. But the more she'd tried to deny it the more convinced Emma had become. She wondered what she would have said if Victoria had told her the truth, that she was being forced into a marriage of convenience with Antonio Cavelli—now she definitely wouldn't believe that!

As she rounded a corner she saw Antonio standing at the far end of the hallway talking to a group of people.

She could hardly believe it herself, she thought nervously.

He didn't notice her immediately and as she walked closer she was able to drink in every detail about him—the immaculate dark business suit that sat so well on his broad shoulders, the pristine white shirt that emphasized his smouldering good looks.

He turned suddenly and as their eyes met she felt her heart starting to slam against her chest like a sledgehammer.

No, Emma would never believe that this handsome Italian was demanding to marry her, because he was completely out of her league. He could have had any woman he set his gaze on. She knew that—was achingly aware that other women were looking in his direction now, and no doubt would do a double take when they saw the plain woman he was marrying.

Not that she cared. She raised her chin defiantly as his dark eyes raked ruthlessly over her appearance. But part of her wanted to turn and run, get out of here while the going was still good. It took all of her courage just to keep putting one foot in front of the other to reach his side.

He smiled. 'Ah, Victoria, perfect timing.' The brisk businesslike tone helped to bring her back to some semblance of sanity—reminded her that her looks were of no concern to him and it really didn't matter that he was out of her league. That basically he regarded her as little more than one of his employees. 'We have some paperwork to complete before we go any further.'

She allowed herself to be guided towards a small side room that contained nothing more than a few chairs and a desk. And then she listened as Antonio introduced her to the two men with him as lawyers; one apparently had been hired especially to represent her and had read through the contracts on her behalf. The other was the Italian solicitor who had drawn them up.

Antonio's gaze drifted over her as she shook hands with the men. Her suit was businesslike but shapeless; for a young woman she was particularly unadventurous when it came to selecting her wardrobe. It was as if she went out of her way to avoid anything that would be in the slightest bit revealing. Still, he wasn't marrying her for her looks or her style, he reminded himself tersely as he pulled out a chair for her. 'Did you read the copy of the prenuptial that I sent over by courier last night?'

She nodded dumbly. She'd forced herself to read the papers in minute detail before going to bed, just in case there was anything in them of any detriment. It had made for sobering reading the night before a wedding, but basically, as far as she could tell, it just set out the terms he had already offered her and stated that she wasn't entitled to anything else in the future.

'And are you happy with everything?' Antonio continued crisply.

The question made Victoria pause for thought. There were a few heartbeats of silence in the room as she looked up at him.

'Well…I don't expect—or want—anything more from you, if that's what you mean,' she answered huskily.

The honesty and vulnerability of her reply made Antonio's dark eyes narrow on her.

One of the lawyers spoke to him in Italian and he pulled his gaze away from her and looked at his watch. Roberto was right—they needed to get a move on; the company jet would be fired up and ready to go in half an hour.

She was getting a good deal—there was nothing more to say, nothing for her really to complain about, he reminded himself briskly. He'd been more than generous with his terms. 'Right, we'll get this signed and then we can move on with the business of the day.'

Someone found a pen for her, and then the papers were placed before her.

Victoria hoped her hands wouldn't shake when she started to sign her name. She felt strangely breathless.

Antonio watched as she tried to settle the little boy on her knee whilst pulling the papers closer.

'Here, let me take the child.' To her dismay he moved closer. 'You can't sign properly like that.'

'No…really, I—'

But Antonio paid her no attention, simply bent and lifted

Nathan easily from her knee. She could smell the delicious aroma of his aftershave, and as his hand brushed accidentally against her body she imagined she could feel his touch burning through the thin cotton material of her jacket.

She glanced at the documents in front of her, her senses in a kind of freefall of chaos.

'That's better.' He held the child casually at his side.

It wasn't better as far as Victoria was concerned. She wanted her son back in her arms, wanted the reassurance and comfort of his little body close to hers. She hoped he would protest, but to her vexation he seemed quite happy.

She took another fleeting look in their direction; in fact, they presented a relaxed portrait that was very much at odds with the reality of the situation. And it suddenly struck her that because Nathan's hair was so dark they could probably pass for father and son. The thought stirred up the strangest of feelings inside of her—feelings that she couldn't even begin to comprehend.

What the hell was wrong with her? she wondered in agitation as she turned her attention back to the papers. Nathan didn't need a father; they were perfectly happy as they were. And even if he did she wouldn't choose someone like Antonio. He was a ruthless businessman, not father material. And anyway, in a few weeks time he would just be a distant memory.

'So where do you want me to sign?' she asked quietly.

One of the lawyers came across and, turning some of the pages, he placed an X in the relevant spaces.

Quickly she scrawled her name and stood just as the receptionist came in to tell them that the registrar was ready any time they were.

Victoria could feel the knot of apprehension inside her tightening.

This was it—once she walked through into the next room she would be giving herself to Antonio Cavelli.

But only for a few weeks, she reminded herself fiercely, and not in any kind of real or meaningful way.

He smiled at her and said something in Italian. The words sounded deliciously romantic and sexy, but of course she knew in reality they would mean something very different, something very practical or even dismissive. Probably something like, *Let's get this over with.*

She swallowed hard. 'I'll take Nathan now.' She reached out for her son, but instead of handing him over Antonio gave him to his lawyer to hold.

'You can have him back in ten minutes when we've exchanged rings and signed the registry.'

'But—'

'Don't look so worried—Roberto is coming inside with us to witness the ceremony.'

'Oh…OK…' She smiled at the child as he held out his arms, wanting to go to her now. 'In a moment, darling…be a good little boy.'

Antonio noticed the tenderness in her voice, the way she reached out and stroked a hand over the child's face.

'Whenever you are ready, Mr Cavelli?' The receptionist was holding the door for them.

'Yes…' Distractedly Antonio glanced back at her. 'Yes…let's get this done. We have a flight to catch.'

CHAPTER FIVE

SHE was exhausted, yet she couldn't sleep. Every time she closed her eyes she could see again the moment when Antonio had taken her hand in his to slip the wedding ring in place. And she remembered how she had felt when she'd looked up at him. The confusing myriad of emotional turmoil was still with her now, whirling around, plaguing her with painful bursts of feelings she couldn't get a handle on.

She twisted the gold band around on her finger; it felt cold and unfamiliar, a little like Antonio's mood since they had been pronounced husband and wife. But then what did she expect? she asked herself angrily—they didn't even know each other. Even a kiss on the cheek and a glass of champagne would be out of place in this scenario. And anyway, even when he momentarily did come too close to her she could feel her whole body stiffen.

After the ceremony when they'd got on board his private jet he'd casually reached to help her adjust her seat belt and she'd frozen. He'd noticed, of course, and had probably found it amusing because he had told her to relax and had then added that he had no intention of eating her.

Ha, ha.

She pressed herself back now into the comfortable leather seat, tried to listen to the drone of the jet engines and allow them to lull her, as they had Nathan. He'd been curled up on the seat beside her, fast asleep, for the past few hours.

She reached out and stroked a stray strand of hair back from his face but he didn't stir. Poor little mite was exhausted. It had been a busy day for him; he'd even missed his usual afternoon nap. Victoria glanced away from the sleeping child over towards the other side of the plane where Antonio was sitting.

He'd been immersed in paperwork since take-off and now he was working on his laptop, the handsome features serious as he studied and made notes. As far as he was concerned the wedding was long forgotten—lost amongst the medley of other business he had to deal with. He could possibly even have forgotten that she was here with him at all, she thought sardonically. Because he hadn't spoken one word to her since take-off.

Well, it suited her.

She just wished that when she closed her eyes she didn't see again the moment when he'd looked at her and pledged to take her for his wife, forsaking all others.

He'd sounded so supremely confident and there had been no other emotion or expression in his voice—but of course there wouldn't have been because he felt nothing, she reminded herself forcefully. The marriage was a sham, a means to an end. She'd noted the vows they made had been carefully selected and cut to avoid promises for a long commitment.

By contrast her voice had been almost a whisper and not in the slightest bit steady. She didn't know why she had felt so...emotional.... After all, she knew the score—she had agreed to the terms.

Her reaction made her feel foolish.

Anyway, it was over now, she told herself fiercely, and it was best forgotten.

He glanced up and as their eyes met she felt the electrical charge of the connection right down to her toes.

'Feeling any better?' he enquired.

'How do you mean?' She frowned.

'You seemed a bit tense earlier,' he remarked casually.

'Did I? I don't know what gave you that idea.' She kept her voice light, desperate to salvage some pride from amongst the fragments of her emotions.

'Good. Ready for something to eat, then.'

It was more statement than question. She watched with a feeling of unease as he closed his laptop and started to clear away the papers on the table in front of him. She wasn't sure she could eat, especially if he expected her to sit opposite him; she felt too wound up.

He glanced over at her again and she swiftly pulled herself together. She couldn't tell him that! 'Yes, OK.'

'Good, I'll call the flight attendant and see what she can rustle up for us.' He pressed the button on the side of his seat. Then indicated to Victoria that she should take the seat opposite him.

'I'll…just freshen up. Will you keep an eye on Nathan for me? His seat belt is secured and I won't be a minute.'

'Sì.' He inclined his head.

Unfastening her seat belt she stood.

'Use the bathroom in the master suite,' he told her as he continued to fold away documents. 'You should find your bag has been placed in there for you.'

'Master suite?' She looked at him in puzzlement and he pointed to a door at the far end of the cabin.

She'd never been on an aircraft like this before in her life. It was weird being the only passengers—a world removed from the economy flight she'd travelled on all those years ago. She opened a door and found herself looking at a large bed.

The place had every modern amenity—wardrobes, and dressing table, and the en-suite bathroom even had a shower.

She went through and closed the door and her reflection stared back at her from the full-length mirror opposite. Her clothes were creased and she looked pale and tired, her hair escaping from the confines of the clips that held it back from her face. Hastily she scraped it back into an even tighter ponytail and then took off her glasses and splashed her face with some cold water.

She wondered if she should change. Her suitcase was fastened onto a stand behind her, and on impulse she opened it. She'd packed a pair of jogging pants and a T-shirt. They would probably be more comfortable to wear now.

Victoria had just finished changing when the plane hit a small pocket of turbulence and her spectacles slid from the vanity unit and hit the floor with a clatter.

Hurriedly she bent to retrieve them. The lenses seemed fine but the arm was hanging off, either the screw had come loose or it had fallen out from the hinge. And as she now couldn't see properly, she couldn't even try to fix it.

The perfect ending to the perfect day, she thought with exasperation. Now everything she looked at was viewed through a slight blur. She wondered if Antonio could mend them for her and then stood indecisively with them in her hand. She didn't want to ask him. But then she hated to be seen without her glasses; she felt naked without them.

The plane hit some more turbulence and it galvanised her into action. It didn't matter about her spectacles; she needed to go back and check that Nathan hadn't woken up. He could be frightened or crying for her.

So glasses in hand she returned to the cabin. By the time she got back, the plane had smoothly levelled out and to her relief Nathan was still fast asleep. Antonio was absorbed in another business report and he didn't look up as she slipped into the seat opposite.

'I took the liberty of ordering dinner for you,' he murmured as he made some notes on the margin of one of the pages. 'Cannelloni followed by beef Wellington. So I hope you are not a vegetarian.'

'No, that's fine.'

'Good.' He continued on with his work.

She watched him through a slight misty haze, then cleared her throat nervously. 'You seem very busy.'

'I've got a lot of Italian business to catch up with, ready for when I get home,' he answered distractedly without looking up.

'When you have a minute…'

'Yes…?'

Still he didn't look up, and he only seemed to be half listening to her. She was quite glad. She didn't want his full attention.

'I dropped my glasses and they…well, they seem to have fallen apart.' *A bit like me,* she thought as he glanced up.

She couldn't see the expression on his face clearly but she was aware that she did have his full attention now, and she could feel her skin starting to tingle with the heat of embarrassment.

'Do you think you could try and fix them for me? I can't see properly, otherwise I'd do it myself.'

Antonio was taken aback for a few moments. She looked totally different. She had rather a lovely shaped face, he thought as he stared at her in startled bemusement. A pert little nose, and high cheekbones that gave her an almost classical beauty. And she looked younger than her years, with skin that was fine grained and smoothly perfect—strange how he hadn't noticed that before. He watched as her long dark lashes swept down over her eyes.

The vulnerability of the look wasn't lost on him.

'Can you fix them for me?' she asked him again huskily. 'Please.'

He took the glasses from her silently and examined them.

The tiny coil that held the hinge in place had slipped and it was a simple matter to just twist it back into position.

'Can you do it?' she asked anxiously as she watched him.

He flicked a glance back over at her; there was a part of him that wanted to say no. A part of him that wanted to say, *Why do you want to hide such a nice face behind such monstrous contraptions?* But then he reminded himself that it was none of his business. She was here for business purposes and to help him teach his father a lesson, nothing more than that. So instead he continued to fix them and slid them back across the table to her. 'Yes, all done.'

'Thanks.'

He watched as she slipped them back on, her manner self-conscious.

The stewardess arrived with their food and the bottle of wine he'd ordered earlier.

'Will there be anything else, sir?' she asked as she efficiently smoothed a white linen tablecloth out and placed crystal glasses and silver cutlery down before them.

'No, that's all for now, thanks, Sally,' he replied as he packed the last of his papers away

'OK, enjoy.' She smiled at him and then with a polite nod in Victoria's direction disappeared.

'Wine?' Antonio lifted the bottle and looked across at her.

'Just a small glass, thanks.'

Victoria watched as he poured the drinks.

The lighting in the cabin was low and the blinds were down on the window beside them. The situation felt strangely intimate—but of course it wasn't, she reminded herself. It was just the weird circumstances. Under normal conditions Antonio probably had a selection of beautiful women whom he would much rather dine with.

The thought made her feel completely ill at ease.

Well, hey, she'd prefer to be anywhere but here herself, she thought fiercely. But they were thirty-nine-thousand feet up in the air and, apart from one sleeping child, quite alone and stuck with each other.

She wished that Nathan would wake up and give her an excuse to escape from the table. She darted a glance over at the child but he was still out for the count.

'Good job you fed him earlier,' Antonio remarked as he caught her glance.

'Yes. He's exhausted.'

'Been a busy day for us all.'

She nodded and looked down at the food in front of her. It looked unexpectedly appetising.

'It won't be as good as the food in your restaurant but it's passable as far as plane food goes,' Antonio told her. 'Try it.'

She did and was pleasantly surprised. 'Last time I ate on a flight, the food tasted like cardboard—but you're right, this isn't bad. The pasta is possibly a little oversalted.'

'Really?' He looked over at her teasingly, and immediately she felt her skin colouring up with heat.

'Sorry—professional habit. I'm afraid cooking for a living tends to turn you into a bit of a food critic.'

He smiled. 'Actually, I think you're right about the pasta.'

'Well, you'd be the expert on that.'

'I suppose I would.' He inclined his head. 'The food in Italy is probably the best in the world. But then I am biased. You can give me your impartial view when we get there.'

'I probably will without even meaning to.'

He studied her quietly for a moment. When she talked about her work and the business of food she was a different woman—more confident, vibrant even. It was as if she only allowed herself to come to life on certain subjects.

What had made her so introverted on a personal level? he wondered.

'So how long have you been running the restaurant?' he asked suddenly.

'About two and a half years.'

'You were pregnant when you started it?'

She nodded but didn't say anything more.

'And you were on your own?'

Again she just gave a nod of her head as an answer.

'That must have been quite tough. Starting a business is daunting even under ordinary circumstances.'

She shrugged, and her emerald-green eyes seemed to flare with fire. 'Nothing worthwhile is easy.'

He knew she was throwing up barriers, that she wanted him to stop questioning her. It was written all over her. But Antonio was not one to back away from something he wanted and he found that, for some reason, he wanted to know what made her tick.

'So what about your child's father…he didn't help you at all?'

For a second Victoria remembered the expression on Lee's handsome face when she'd told him she was pregnant. *'You'll just have to get rid of it. You didn't think I would want it, did you…? Hell, Vicky, you were only ever a one-night fling.'*

The memory made her go cold inside. OK, she'd only slept with Lee once but he had taken her out for a few months before that night of madness.

After they'd slept together he hadn't contacted her again and she'd realized that one night was all he had wanted. But she'd still believed she had a duty to tell him she was pregnant. That he had a right to know that he would be a father. She hadn't expected anything from him, but such cold dismissal had been a shock.

She should never have got involved with him in the first place, should have known better. She had been naive and foolish back then, desperately looking for love and affection in the wrong place.

Well, she'd learnt her lesson about that.

'I take it he didn't want to know when you told him you were pregnant?'

The question was too much.

Antonio saw the glimmer of raw pain in her eyes, before it was quickly veiled behind dark lashes.

'That's really none of your business, is it?' She said the words quietly. Yet her voice was filled with dignity. 'You and I are married as part of a…a deal. And that deal doesn't give you the right to question my morals or my life choices.'

'You're right, it doesn't.'

'So don't!' Again there was that fulminating glare from eyes that were ice green now, extraordinary eyes, almost catlike.

'For what it's worth, my moral judgement was falling quite heavily on the guy who chose to walk away from his child,' Antonio told her softly. 'But you're right, it's none of my business.'

The door opened into the cabin and the stewardess came over to them. 'Is everything all right with the meal, sir? Are you ready for your main course?'

Antonio glanced over at Victoria and she nodded. 'Yes, I'm finished, thanks.'

There was silence as the appetizers were cleared away. Antonio noticed that Victoria hadn't eaten much at all.

More silver salvers were placed in front of them and then they were left alone again.

'Let's hope the beef is properly seasoned,' Antonio said wryly. 'Otherwise when we land to refuel in Hong Kong we might have to send out for a Chinese meal.'

The statement was so absurd that Victoria laughed, then darted him a curious look. 'That was a joke, right?'

'Yes, it was.' He smiled. 'But if you'd like Chinese it could be arranged. We land in a few hours.'

'I love Chinese food. But I'll stick with the beef Wellington.'

'You haven't tasted it yet.' He leaned over and topped up her glass. 'So when was the last time you had aeroplane food?' he asked casually.

She flicked him a wary look.

'You were telling me earlier about it tasting like cardboard,' he prompted.

'It was a long time ago when I was flying from London to Sydney. I was fourteen.' She cut into the beef and found it was perfectly cooked. 'I don't really remember what I ate, but I do remember it was not as good as this.'

'I thought your accent was more English than Australian. I take it you were immigrating to Australia with your parents?'

'I was on my own actually. My mother had just died and I was sent to live with her sister.'

'And where was your father?'

'He'd died a year earlier.' She looked over at him. 'You'll be happy to know that the food is perfectly seasoned. So no need for that Chinese.'

He noticed the swift change of tack and knew it was deliberate, knew that she really didn't want to talk about herself at all. And he supposed he had no right to pry; as she'd already so concisely told him, her personal life was none of his business.

'Your life must be amazing,' she murmured suddenly.

'Must it?' He looked over at her with a glimmer of amusement in his dark eyes.

'Yes…I mean to be so rich and so powerful that you can have anything you want, whenever you want it. That's pretty amazing.'

'I've never really thought about it like that. I'm always too busy working.' He took a sip of his wine and sat back in the comfortable leather chair. 'But yes, I suppose wealth does have a lot of pluses.'

'What's the most impetuous thing you've ever done?' she asked curiously.

'You mean apart from buying myself a wife?'

He looked at her wryly and she could feel the heat of humiliation seeping over her body. She supposed he *had* bought her. And when she allowed herself to think about it in those terms, it was absolutely mortifying.

'You know, I don't think I am hungry after all.' She put the cutlery down with a clatter. She wanted to get away from him. She couldn't sit here and smile politely and pretend that she was all right with what she'd done. *With what he had forced her to do,* she reminded herself fiercely. Because he was the one who'd made sure she'd run out of options. 'If you'll excuse me, I think I'll—'

'Sit down,' he said quietly as she started to rise to her feet.

She paid him no attention and he reached across and caught hold of her arm. It was only the briefest of contacts, but it made her senses go into freefall.

'Sit down,' he said again.

The low commanding tone wasn't one to argue with. Slowly she did as she was told and sank back into the chair.

'You asked me a question and I gave you the honest answer. I've taken you as my wife as part of a business deal—it is pretty extreme.'

She tried to shrug as if she didn't care, and from somewhere she found the resources within her to try and joke. 'Well, let's hope I'm value for money.'

He watched how she angled her chin up. She was a very intriguing blend of vulnerability and feisty defiance, he thought distractedly.

'So far, I think I've got a good deal.' There was a teasing gleam in the darkness of his eyes as he smiled lazily at her. 'But time will tell.'

She wished he wouldn't look at her like that! Or say things like that. It made her feel weird inside—scared and...totally keyed up. 'Time will tell with what...exactly?'

'With how you perform in Italy.'

'Perform?' Her eyes narrowed on him warily.

'Well, I shall require some wifely duties from you, Victoria,' Antonio told her. 'But nothing more rigorous than accompanying me for dinner at my father's house. He'll be anxious to meet you.'

'I see...' She frowned, but didn't really understand. 'So have you told him that the marriage is...a sham?'

'The marriage is real, Victoria, and I have the certificate to prove it.' For a moment the darkness of his eyes seemed to cut through her. 'But no, he doesn't know anything about you or about our arrangement—not yet anyway.' He was saving that revelation for when he could see him face to face.

Victoria noticed the expression of determination on

Antonio's face now, a look that made her wonder what was going on between him and his father. 'And you're looking forward to telling him...aren't you?' she whispered.

The gently perceptive remark made him focus on her again. 'Yes, Victoria, I'm looking forward to that moment very much.'

She wanted to ask why but she didn't dare go any further, because there was a cool aura of authority about him that seemed to forbid it.

Silence fell between them and she picked up her cutlery again and tried to eat a few more mouthfuls, but it was a relief when the stewardess finally returned to clear the table and she could allow her to take the plate away.

Antonio ordered a black coffee, but Victoria declined anything else.

He leaned back and let his eyes drift over her thoughtfully.

'I wish you wouldn't look at me like that!' she murmured impulsively.

'Like what?' He seemed amused by the remark.

'I don't know...' She shrugged helplessly. All she knew was that when his eyes drifted slowly over her it made strange little shivers pierce straight through her body. But then that was probably more to do with her than him, she realized with acute embarrassment. 'I guess...I'm just tired.' Clumsily she tried to cover the words. 'How much longer, before we reach our destination?'

'Only about another nineteen hours or so.'

Her heart seemed to plunge somewhere down into her stomach.

He smiled. 'You need to relax.'

How could she relax when he could churn her emotions to shreds with just one look! 'Yes, I think I'll go and sit back beside Nathan now.' She flicked an unconsciously pleading glance across the table, willing him to allow her to escape. 'If I may?' She added the question pointedly as she remembered how he had commanded her to stay where she was.

'You may do as you please,' he told her sardonically. Her reaction to him bemused him slightly; there weren't many women who ran away from him. 'Maybe you'd like to make yourself more comfortable in the bedroom? See if you can get some sleep.'

'That would be great, but what about you?' She asked the question without thinking, and it was only when she saw the gleam in his eye that she realized it could be misconstrued.

'Is that an invitation?' he asked lazily.

'No! You know very well that it wasn't!'

Obviously she was completely mortified. He couldn't remember the last time a woman had blushed like that when he'd teased. Her shy manner really was quite delightful.

'I was just checking that you don't want to take the room for yourself, that's all!' she continued hurriedly.

'Very considerate of you.' He smiled. 'And I assure you, if I want to stake my claim on anything I'll let you know a little later on. But right now, I have some more work to catch up on.'

He was just bantering with her, she realized suddenly. Trouble was, she really couldn't think straight around him— he totally flustered her.

She wondered suddenly what it would be like to have him *really* flirt with her, as if he were *really* interested in her. The thought made her emotions flip wildly and quickly she pushed it away, because even thinking along those lines was storing up danger.

Antonio was the type of man who would flirt without even a moment realizing he was doing it. And he would never be serious about someone like her.

'Well, I'll leave you to your work.' Hastily she turned away. 'And I'll bring Nathan into the other room with me, in case he disturbs you.'

'Whatever suits you.'

What suited her was getting away from him as fast as

possible. Even when he looked at her with amusement in his eyes, it made her senses spin.

Victoria got to her feet and reached into an overhead locker to get Nathan's bag but it was wedged firmly into the tight space and she found it difficult to pull it free. She stood on tiptoe and tugged a little harder.

Antonio found himself watching her.

The loose T-shirt she wore was raised by the way her arms were reaching up, giving him his first clear view of her small waist. He found himself noticing how the tightly fitting pants she wore emphasized a flat stomach and a well-rounded pert derrière that was surprisingly provocative. His gaze moved over her slowly, and then lingered on the shapeless T-shirt, wondering what her breasts were like.

He frowned to himself.

It didn't matter what her breasts were like, he reminded himself quickly. She wasn't his type and he didn't want to make this situation any more complicated than it already was.

Victoria tugged even more frantically on the strap of the bag. She was overly conscious now of the fact that Antonio was getting to his feet.

'Do you need some help?' He folded away the table in front of him to make more room.

'No, thanks, I'm managing.' She said the words with a kind of gritted determination that made him smile, and he moved towards her anyway.

'Really, I'm managing.' She flicked a nervous glance over her shoulder. But he paid her no attention and moved behind her to stretch over her head and lift the bag easily down.

He didn't touch her, but in the confined space his body was just a whisper away from hers, so close that he could almost feel the tension in her, emanating like an invisible barrier. It was strange he'd never known a woman to respond to him the way she did. Usually women flirted coyly with him, or moved deliberately closer if they got the chance. Victoria by contrast seemed petrified of making any contact with him whatsoever. She almost seemed to freeze.

His gaze moved down over the slender vulnerable column of her neck.

Her reserve suited him, he reminded himself. It was part of the reason why she was the perfect wife of convenience. It meant no complications, no emotional minefields.

'Is this all you want from the locker? There are some toys in there too.'

'I just need the bag. Thanks.' She wanted to turn and take it from him but she didn't dare until he moved back from her. And he seemed in no hurry to do that. Instead he reached around her and placed it on the seat in front of her. The movement brought him closer, his arm brushing against hers. She could feel the warmth of his breath against her neck and it sent quivers of reaction rushing through her.

If he hadn't known better he would have sworn she was a virgin, Antonio thought suddenly. She was so unworldly— aeons and light years away from the sophisticated women who gave themselves to him so freely without even a second thought.

He wondered what would happen if he pulled her back into his arms. She'd probably be terrified. For a second he imagined turning her around...claiming her mouth in a pos- sessive kiss, her lips trembling and softly pliant. She would be unschooled in the art of lovemaking.

But of course she wasn't! She had a child. And what the hell was he thinking?

He frowned and moved away from her. OK, she had a naivety about her that intrigued him, but he wasn't interested. And he really was going to have to stop analysing her, because she was acquired for business purposes only, and if he over- stepped the line in any way, it would be a mistake.

Antonio was very careful about the women he got involved with because he knew he was incapable of settling down. But at least he understood that about himself. At least he only dated women who were sophisticated and experienced, women who knew the score and wouldn't get hurt. His one horror in life would be that he turned into his father.

He returned to his seat and was just about to refasten his safety belt when the plane hit some turbulence and Victoria stumbled backwards. For a moment the whole cabin seemed to tilt and instinctively Antonio reached out and grabbed her around the waist.

It was all over within a second and as the aircraft levelled out Victoria found herself sitting on Antonio's knee, his hands spanning her tiny waist, holding her tightly and protectively against him.

The shock of finding herself in such an *intimate* situation was intense. She was absolutely horrified. 'Sorry...I...I fell.'

'Yes, so I gathered.' He was momentarily amused.

Her body felt surprising good against his, warm and curvaceous. He could smell the clean scent of shampoo from her hair and the honeyed undertones of her perfume. He held her closer as the plane shuddered violently once more and he realized suddenly that his hands were touching her bare skin now, and that he could feel her ribs beneath his fingers, could feel the satin softness of her.

'I'll be okay now...' Suddenly she was scrabbling to get away from him even though the plane wasn't entirely steady—and he could tell that her skin was on fire.

She was attracted to him, he realized suddenly. And if he wanted to he could pull her back against him, explore her curves more thoroughly. For a moment the idea was tantalizing. Then he pulled himself up in annoyance. OK, her unsophisticated naivety was refreshing but it certainly wasn't for him. And he wasn't going to do anything so crazy.

'Do you want me to help you to move Nathan?'

Hurriedly she shook her head. The memory of his hands against her skin was still sizzling inside her with disturbing intensity and the thought of him accompanying her into the bedroom made her heart smash against her chest with even more force.

'No, I'll manage, thanks.'

'OK.' He returned his attention to the work he had put away. But out of the corner of his eye he was aware that she was lifting up the sleeping child.

The stewardess returned with his coffee as Victoria disappeared through to the master suite, closing the door firmly behind her.

That was better, Antonio told himself fiercely.

CHAPTER SIX

THEY landed in Hong Kong in the early hours of the morning. It was a quick stop, probably no more than forty minutes. Victoria rolled over in the double bed and pulled the blind on the window up a little to take a peek outside but she could see nothing except the orange lights of workmen. A little while later the engines fired up again and once more they were thundering down the runway.

It was a strange experience to lie in bed with the seat belts firmly fastened over her as the plane took off and soared higher and higher into the darkness of the sky, the air currents shaking the cabin from time to time and the powerful engines roaring.

Despite the sleeping child next to her, she felt lonely, terrified of what might lie ahead. But she was being ridiculous, she told herself fiercely—there was nothing to worry about.

Once they reached Antonio's house she probably wouldn't see a lot of him. He'd probably be away at his office all day. And she'd have time to spend with Nathan.

She closed her eyes again and remembered the moment when she'd fallen back onto his knee. Remembered the powerful electrical feeling of desire as his hands touched her skin. The memory taunted her...made her shiver deep inside with feelings that scared her to death. Fiercely she tried to block the thoughts, hating herself for the weakness. It had just been a crazy unreal moment—she'd imagined the way he'd made her feel. Just as she'd imagined for one wild instant that he might have been tempted to pull her closer, touch her more intimately.

She almost laughed at the stupidity of the thought. This was the man who could have anything he wanted whenever he wanted, including his pick of the world's most beautiful women. And he had made it crystal clear to her that she was nothing to him, a mere belonging, acquired at a price…and for business, not for pleasure.

The aircraft levelled out as they reached the required altitude and the seat-belt sign went off.

She felt heart sore and exhausted, the emotions of the day tumbling around and around inside of her.

The next moment she had fallen fast asleep.

Strange dreams plagued her—dreams where she was walking down a church aisle to marry Antonio, and she was wearing a beautiful wedding dress. Dreams where they danced together at a party, Antonio pulling her closer in against him.

'You want me, don't you?' he whispered mockingly.

She tried to say no but the word kept sticking in her throat and that made him laugh at her.

She tried to pull away from him but he was going to kiss her, and strangely her body wouldn't move. She wanted him to kiss her, wanted to feel the heat of his mouth on hers—the mere thought made her dissolve inside with pleasure. But when she raised her eyes to look up at him she discovered that it wasn't Antonio holding her, that it was Lee who was staring down at her, his lips curved in cruel mocking smile.

She awoke with a start, her heart thumping wildly against her chest.

For a moment the dream felt real…. She was in a complete panic.

She took deep breaths and forced herself to relax. It was

just a stupid nightmare, she told herself. Lee was long gone—and as for this marriage with Antonio…it would be over in a matter of weeks. There would be no chance of him holding her or kissing her…*or hurting her*. Neither of them wanted that complication.

She sat up and looked over at Nathan. The boy was just waking up and he had kicked back the covers she had placed over him and was trying his best to wriggle out from the safety belt that held him.

'Hey, little devil, what are you up to?' She rolled over and playfully tickled him and he laughed, his little legs kicking out even harder.

'I know what you want—you want your breakfast, don't you?' She put her arms around her son and cuddled him closer, but he pulled away and gave an impatient little cry. Hunger was taking him over and Victoria knew that if he didn't get his breakfast soon tears would closely follow.

'OK, point taken.' She smiled and unfastened her own safety belt and got up.

She would have liked to take a shower and wash her hair before going out into the main cabin but she knew from experience that she had to feed Nathan first, otherwise he would turn from sunny-natured into a loud and very rebellious grouchy child. So she reached for her dressing gown and tried to tidy her hair as best she could.

Nathan was giving little whimpers now, so she didn't loiter on her appearance, just gathered the fractious child up into her arms and headed out into the main cabin.

She half expected Antonio to be asleep. But as she glanced down the plane she saw that he was still working on some papers, his head bent. Had he worked all night? she wondered in surprise.

Luckily she didn't have to go down past him; the small galley kitchen that she had used to prepare Nathan's dinner yesterday was just to her left. Hastily she busied herself, plugging in the kettle and opening the fridge to find the banana, cereal and milk that she had placed in there yesterday. Nathan's little wails of protest were starting to get louder and she spoke to him soothingly as she worked.

Antonio heard them before he saw them and put his papers down to glance further along the plane.

The sun was slanting in through the cabin windows, catching mother and child in a shaft of bright light. They made an intriguing picture of domesticity. She was wearing a long blue satin dressing gown and her hair was cascading in glossy waves around her shoulders. He hadn't realized how lovely her hair was, or how long it was.

She looked very feminine and startlingly different…and for a moment he couldn't take his eyes off her.

Then he was distracted by the stewardess coming out to ask him if he wanted anything, and by the time he glanced back up towards the galley she was gone.

He'd probably imagined it, he told himself wryly, just as he'd imagined a sensual pleasure when he'd momentarily held her close. Victoria was many things—she was interesting and certainly different, and without her glasses passably attractive—but there was no wow factor. And he certainly wasn't attracted to her.

Victoria didn't re-emerge again until the pilot announced that they were starting to make their final descent into Brescia Airport. Antonio was quietly relieved when he saw her walking down the aisle towards him, Nathan at her hip, because she was once more the staid woman he had first met at the restaurant. Her dark hair neatly scraped back from a face that was far too pale and dominated by glasses, wearing a rather shapeless black trouser suit that did nothing for her. He smiled to himself—obviously he had worked far too hard last night and had been hallucinating when he'd thought she looked beautiful.

'How was the bed—did you sleep OK?' he asked her solicitously as she reached his side.

'Yes, it was very comfortable, thank you.' She tried to smile but she was achingly self-conscious.

'You need to sit down and fasten your seat belt—we're nearly home.'

The words spoken with the warmth of his Italian accent were disorientating. But this wasn't home, she reminded herself quickly as she slipped into the seat diagonally opposite him beside the window; this was just another stopgap in her life. She fastened Nathan into the seat beside her and then focused her attention out of the window.

Antonio found himself facing Nathan. And as their eyes met across the table the little boy smiled at him disarmingly. He was really quite a cute little fellow, Antonio thought distractedly. And Victoria seemed to spend more money and time on his appearance than she did with her own. The clothes he wore looked like a latest design and brand new. Not that he knew much about kids or their clothes, he realized. In fact, he'd never had much to do with children at all. He probably just wasn't the paternal type; some people weren't. Certainly the thought of getting it wrong and messing some poor child's life up because he had commitment issues was scary in the extreme.

The pilot spoke over the intercom, telling them they were twenty minutes away from landing. Victoria was waiting for her first glimpse of Italy, excitement swirling inside of her, but for a while she could see nothing but clouds. Then the plane dipped and she had her first clear view of the landscape. The sun was shining and everything looked dazzlingly green and lush. She could see rolling vineyards and mountains, tiny roads weaving between fields of grain.

The engine noises increased and they were coming lower now, and a few minutes later the wheels touched smoothly down on the runway and the engine roared as the speed was pulled back.

Victoria glanced over at Nathan to make sure he wasn't

scared, but he looked delighted and was taking everything in with great interest.

'I think your son is going to be a pilot when he grows up,' Antonio told her as he caught her eye. 'He seems to love flying.'

She laughed. 'He likes anything that involves speed—he's absolutely crazy about racing cars too.'

'Really.' Antonio smiled at the child, then reached across to ruffle his hair. 'I can see you are going to fit in very well around here, *bambino*.'

It was the first time that Antonio had acknowledged Nathan like that, the first time he had looked in any way interested in her child.

And for some reason it smote at Victoria's heart.

He glanced over and caught her watching him, and quickly she looked away.

What on earth was the matter with her? she wondered angrily. Nathan wasn't going to fit in around here any more than she was, because they were both outsiders, and in a few weeks would be surplus to requirements. And that was the way she wanted it, because the sooner this ridiculous marriage was over, and the sooner she gained control of her life again, the better.

They'd hardly spoken a word since they'd climbed into the limousine at the airport. Victoria sat on one side of the car, Nathan on her knee, and Antonio sat at the other.

Victoria wondered if it was her imagination or was the tension between them worse now that they were actually here. Maybe Antonio regretted this hasty marriage.

She darted a glance around at him, but his features were stern and determined as he looked ahead. And she almost laughed at herself. Antonio wasn't the type of man to have regrets. He was too full of arrogant self-confidence.

She looked away again. The narrow road was following

along beside a lake that was so large Victoria thought it was the sea for a moment. Then they were driving through some spectacular mountainous scenery, the road winding and twisting with steep drops at one side. She had a sudden glimpse of a village perched on the other side of the lake. It looked medieval, like a picture from a Hans Christian Andersen fairy tale, the tangled riot of red roofs contrasting starkly with the sheer rocky cliffs that soared behind it.

'This place is beautiful,' she spoke impulsively, and Antonio looked around.

'It's called Limone,' he informed her briskly. 'The Italian word for lemons—the shore is renowned for its citrus trees. However, the name doesn't originate from the trees but from an older Latin word meaning boundary.'

'You know a lot about it.'

He smiled at that. 'I should think so. The Cavelli family go back for many generations around here. Lake Garda is practically in the blood.' He leaned forward and spoke in Italian to their driver and at the first opportunity he pulled into the side of the road.

'Do you see that place down there?' Antonio pointed through the tracery of trees down towards the water and she saw a mansion jutting out by the shoreline. Its huge stone walls were crenulated, its windows staring out blankly across the stillness of the blue water. 'That is my ancestral home.'

Victoria's eyes widened. 'It looks more like a castle!'

'Yes, the family always did have grand ideas.' Antonio's voice was almost derisive. 'My father lives there. I was brought up by my mother in a smaller, more modest house further along the shore—that is where I am taking you now.'

'So your parents don't live together?'

'They separated when I was ten. But my mother is dead now,' he continued. 'She died years ago.'

Antonio spoke in Italian to the driver and they pulled out onto the road again.

'So your parents were divorced?' Victoria gathered the courage to try and continue the conversation, curious to know more about his life.

'No, my father didn't believe in divorce,' Antonio grated the words derisively. 'He preferred the excitement of infidelity.'

The curt reply took her by surprise and was somehow probably more revealing than he would have wanted it to be. 'You don't sound as if you like your father very much.'

'We tolerate each other.'

She noticed how closed his handsome features were now. 'That's sad…don't you think?'

For a second he looked at her and frowned, as if the question startled him. 'No, Victoria, I think it's just a reality.'

The car stopped again but this time it was to wait for huge electric gates to grind slowly open.

Then they drove down along a gravel driveway through cypress trees and manicured gardens until it revealed a huge sprawling white house that was snuggled securely into the curve of the lake.

'If you think this is a modest house, then it's no wonder you thought my apartment was small,' she said impulsively.

He laughed at that and opened the door into the warmth of the Italian day. 'Come inside and make yourself at home.'

A middle-aged woman met them at the door. Victoria gathered that she was the housekeeper, and that her name was Sarah, but apart from that she couldn't understand anything because the conversation that flowed so rapidly around her was all in Italian.

She did comprehend, however, that the woman was visibly surprised when Antonio introduced her as his wife. Her eyes raked over Victoria, and then lingered on the child in her arms with considerable consternation. Probably thinking that she wasn't Antonio's type.

Well, she didn't care, Victoria told herself fiercely as she lifted her chin and met the woman's cool appraisal head-on.

'Show Signora Cavelli up to her room, please, Sarah,' Antonio told the woman in crisp Italian.

'You mean to your room?' the housekeeper questioned.

'No, I mean the adjoining room—the one I asked you to make up when I spoke to you on the phone yesterday.' Antonio's voice was rigid now with annoyance. Sarah had worked in this house for nearly twenty years and he was fond of her, but she had no right to question him and to look so damn disapproving! He would do as he pleased...marry who he damn well pleased. 'And did you arrange for that merchandise I asked for to be delivered—the cot, et cetera?'

'Yes, it's all in the room.'

'Good—well, then, you know where my wife is sleeping, don't you?' Antonio threw her a pointed look and then glanced at his watch impatiently. 'I've phone calls to make. I'll be in my study.' He had no more time to waste on this.

Antonio was about to turn and just march away when he noticed how apprehensive Victoria looked, how tightly she was holding onto the child in her arms. Anyone would think he had delivered her into the depths of hell!

'Go and relax. I'll see you later, Victoria,' he told her dismissively.

She angled her chin higher as if to say, *Don't bother,* and he found himself smiling as he turned away.

'Take good care of her, Sarah.' He threw the Italian command almost carelessly over his shoulder, but this time his voice was gentle. 'Make sure she has everything she needs.'

'Yes...of course.' The woman watched him walk away, a look of perplexity in her eyes now, and Victoria wondered what Antonio had said to her.

She wished with all her heart that she spoke Italian.

The chauffeur came in with the luggage and Sarah turned towards the stairs. 'Come this way,' she told Victoria in stiff English.

The house was spectacular, Victoria thought as she

followed the woman silently up along the grand sweeping staircase and along the wide corridors.

The bedroom she was shown into was the largest and most luxurious room she had ever been in. She gasped in surprise as her eyes moved over the enormous four-poster bed, the sumptuous cream brocade furnishings and the window that led out to a small balcony that overlooked the bright blue sparkle of the lake.

'Is this room really for me?' She stood just inside the doorway, looking around her as if it had all been a huge mistake and she should really have been shown to the staff quarters.

'Yes.' The housekeeper gave her a grudging smile and opened the door into the en-suite bathroom. 'You'll find all the towels you need in the cabinet. There is also a selection of toiletries in there—so help yourself.'

'Thank you.' She stood awkwardly as the chauffeur placed her bags down beside the bed. She couldn't help noticing how shabby her luggage looked amidst such grand surroundings and she was well aware that the housekeeper had observed the same.

'The child's nursery is through here.' Sarah opened up another door to reveal a large airy room that contained a stylish cot with a pretty blue mobile of sailing ships hanging over it.

Victoria walked slowly over to have a closer look. Everything about the room was luxurious. The bedding on the cot was exquisitely embroidered and there was a comfortable armchair that was upholstered in matching fabric placed by the window. A selection of bedtime storybooks sat on a table, and stacked up on a shelf there was everything she would need for Nathan—a baby listening device, even a selection of clothes and various creams and baby lotions. 'Does someone in Antonio's family have a child?' she asked the housekeeper in perplexity. She hadn't expected anything like this.

'Sì.' Sarah frowned. 'Yes…*you*.'

'But…' Victoria had been going to say that she was just a temporary guest but one look at the woman's face made her shut up.

'The *signor* told me to get everything a two-year-old little boy would need.' She swept a hand around the room. 'I have done my best.'

'Thank you, it's wonderful.' The room overwhelmed her—she'd never had a nursery for Nathan before; he'd always slept in his cot next to her bed. She remembered that when she'd been pregnant she'd occasionally flicked wistfully through the magazines on motherhood to look at the pretty photographs of nurseries like this, remembered wishing…

Aware suddenly that the housekeeper was watching her, she pulled herself together. 'And…what's through here?' She pointed to another door next the one that led through to the nursery.

'That one, *signora*, leads through to your husband's quarters.'

Victoria had been about to open the door and she quickly allowed her hand to drop from the handle. 'Oh, I see…' She could feel herself starting to heat up with embarrassment as she met the other woman's eyes. 'Well…thank you once again for arranging such a lovely room for me.'

'You're welcome.' The woman smiled for a moment. 'Can I get you anything else, Signora Cavelli?'

The suddenly respectful tone in the other woman's voice took her by surprise, as did her title, but then she supposed that was her name—for now.

'No, thank you, I have everything I need.'

The woman nodded and walked briskly away. 'Dinner will be served at eight in the main dining room,' she said and closed the door firmly behind her.

Victoria sat down on the bed. She felt exhausted suddenly, which was strange because even though they'd made a long journey she'd slept for quite a while on the plane. Nathan on the other hand seemed filled with energy and wiggled impatiently to get down from her knee. She allowed him to slip to the floor and then watched as he toddled around the room to explore.

'Don't touch the mirror, Nat,' she told him as he put little fingers all over the mirrored wardrobes opposite.

He looked around at her and smiled, then moved on and found her suitcase and tried to unfasten it.

But Victoria's gaze was locked on her appearance in the mirror.

The suit she was wearing had seen better days, her skin was deathly pale and she looked drawn and anxious. It was no wonder that the housekeeper had looked taken aback when Antonio had introduced her as his wife.

It would only have taken one glance for the woman to know that she clearly didn't belong here.

Nathan was trying unsuccessfully to unfasten the side pockets of the bag now and she stood from the bed and went across to pick him up.

It didn't matter what anyone else thought because she didn't care, she reminded herself again as she gathered up his bag and headed through to the nursery.

Her priority was her child.

But then surprisingly Antonio seemed to have considered him a priority too, she thought as she looked around at the things that had been purchased especially for her child.

The man was full of surprises.

Nathan wanted to get down—he'd seen the box of toys at the far side of the room and he was eager to explore.

Normally at this time he'd have been getting sleepy but clearly his body clock was confused with the travel and time change.

Maybe some fresh air would help, she thought as she glanced out of the window at the spectacular view. In fact, maybe some fresh air would help both of them.

CHAPTER SEVEN

ANTONIO stepped out of the shower and dressed in a hurry. He had spent two solid hours on the phone to his office in Verona and he was still going to have to drive over there tonight to sort out some paperwork for the morning.

After such a long flight it was a damn inconvenience, plus he'd been hoping to meet with his father tonight to impart his good news. Antonio's lips twisted derisively. Ah, well, that particular pleasure would have to be savoured tomorrow evening now. He'd already rung to whet the old man's curiosity—had told him he wished to discuss the details of his business deal and that he had brought someone home with him.

His father had been absolutely delighted, and had immediately invited him and his guest over for dinner—had been most disappointed when Antonio had told him that it would now have be tomorrow due to pressure of work.

'So who have you brought home with you, Antonio?' he had asked gleefully.

'You'll have to wait and see, Father,' he had told him, his voice carefully neutral. 'But as I am complying with your wishes, I will of course expect you to keep to your side of the agreement.'

'Of course, next year, once you are married and your son or daughter comes along, I shall be more than happy to retire and hand my shares in the company over to you.'

Antonio smiled to himself now as he fastened his blue silk tie. His father would be retiring next week, not next year, he thought with satisfaction. And it was going to feel very sweet. The man would rue the day he had ever tried to force his will upon him. With impatient fingers he reached for his suit jacket before glancing at his watch. It was almost six in the evening now and once he'd sorted things out in the office it wouldn't be worth driving back here again tonight. Far more convenient to stay at his apartment in town, he decided as he picked up his overnight bag and some keys before heading out of his room.

Sarah was downstairs in the hallway polishing the brass handles on the front door. 'I won't be home for dinner, Sarah, and I shall be staying at my apartment in town overnight,' he told her briskly.

'Very well, *signor.*' She didn't look around.

'Tell Signora Cavelli that I will see her tomorrow. We have been invited to my father's house for dinner so she should make herself and the child ready to leave at seven o'clock.'

'Very well.' The woman glanced over at him now. 'But if you would like to tell her yourself, you will find her out in the garden. She is taking some fresh air with her son.'

'I have no time,' he retorted brusquely. 'So just give her the message, Sarah.'

The woman nodded, a look of stern disapproval in her eyes. 'She seems a nice girl.'

Antonio shrugged.

The woman arched one eyebrow and he smiled. 'I'll see you tomorrow. Just remember…I want to be the first to break the happy news to my father tomorrow evening.'

'You don't need to remind me about things like that!' The woman put one hand on her ample hip and glared at him indignantly. 'I've always been the soul of discretion.'

'Indeed.' Antonio nodded. He knew Sarah was trustworthy—however, the reminder didn't hurt. He stepped past her and went outside.

The sun was starting to go down, leaving a blazing trail of red and gold over the tranquil surface of the lake. The evening was warm and mellow and the beauty of his surroundings enveloped him as his footsteps crunched over the gravel towards his car. Sometimes he forgot how lovely this place was, he thought, pausing briefly to look around him.

At the far end of the lawn he caught sight of Victoria. She was playing ball with her son, throwing it gently for him and then clapping her hands as he caught it and tried to throw it back.

'Clever boy…' Her laughter drifted on the warmth of the evening, and despite the fact that he was on limited time, Antonio found himself watching her. She was wearing a faded pair of blue denim jeans with a loose-fitting checked shirt. And although her hair was pulled back from her face it was secured in a silky ponytail that had flicked over one shoulder and fell almost to her waist.

'Catch, Nathan, catch…' The child dissolved into giggles as he missed the ball and then he ran after it as fast as his little legs would carry him, his mother pretending to give chase.

Antonio smiled to himself as she caught the little boy easily and swung him off his feet and around and around in the air. There was something about the happy carefree moment that was somehow touching—why that was he didn't know, he thought with irritation. He was about to turn away when she caught sight of him.

Immediately he saw the tension return to the slender lines of her body.

She looked like a gazelle about to take flight from a hungry predator. What the hell did she think he was going to do to her? he wondered in irritation as he unlocked his car.

'Are you going out?' she called rather breathlessly to him. Surprised by the question he glanced around and found she was heading slowly towards him, carrying the child on her hip.

'Yes. I have things to do.' He tossed his overnight bag into the boot of the red sports car. Then aware that she was still standing a few feet away watching him, he turned and looked at her again. 'Was there something you wanted, Victoria?'

The cool enquiry made her feel awkward. 'Well…'

He glanced at his watch. 'Because if not, I'm a very busy man.'

'I just wanted to say thank-you,' she cut across him swiftly.

'For what?' He frowned.

'For going to so much trouble to get the room ready for Nathan.' She was regarding him steadily, as if forcing herself to make eye contact.

'Oh, that.' He shrugged. 'Believe me, it wasn't any trouble. I just delegated the task to Sarah.'

'Yes…but it was still good of you. All those toys and that equipment must have cost a fortune and…well, the room is beautiful. I've never had a nursery for Nathan.'

For some reason the touching sincerity of her words prickled uncomfortably inside him. 'I don't want your thanks, Victoria,' he told her abruptly. 'I said I'd look after you and Nathan whilst you are under my roof and I'm a man of my word. All I require from you is that you keep to your side of the deal, that you don't get in my way and that you make yourself available when I want you.'

'I'll…do my best.' She took a step away from him as if half scared by his words, her cheeks flaring with colour.

'My father has invited us for dinner tomorrow. Sarah will give you details.'

She watched helplessly as he started to turn away. 'And is it okay to bring Nathan…? It's just that I don't want to leave him… I—'

'Yes, of course you must bring Nathan.' He frowned as if the question was completely stupid. 'I wouldn't hear of leaving him!'

'Wouldn't you?' She looked at him in bewilderment.

'No, now if that's all you wanted I have to go—'

'OK, oh, just one more thing… What do you want me to

wear?' She asked the question impulsively before he could climb into the car.

'To wear?' He turned slowly and looked at her as if the question amused him.

'Yes, what form of dress is appropriate?' She shrugged, feeling horrendously embarrassed now. But she'd rather have asked him than risk asking the disapproving housekeeper who would probably sneer down her nose at her. 'It's just…I didn't bring much with me and—'

'It doesn't matter what you wear, Victoria,' he cut across her dismissively. 'Wear anything—wear that suit that you wore for our wedding ceremony,' he suggested offhandedly.

His eyes raked over her, noticing how her blouse was pulled tight across her chest by the way she was holding Nathan. And for a moment he remembered the way her body had felt against his when she had stumbled onto his knee on the plane. The memory made him tense. Why the hell was he thinking about that? he wondered angrily. This was about business! 'Yes, in fact, that suit will be perfect,' he said resolutely as he remembered how plain she had looked in it.

'Really?' She frowned. The suit was nowhere near perfect and she was well aware of that fact. She'd chosen it for the ceremony more as an act of defiance than anything else.

However, why should she care? she wondered suddenly. It wasn't as if she needed to make a good impression on his father. It wasn't as if she was a real daughter-in-law. She wouldn't be around for long anyway. 'OK,' she murmured. 'If you think it's suitable.'

'Most suitable.' He nodded. 'And wear your hair the way it was for the ceremony as well…' His eyes flicked over her. 'Yes, it's much better completely back from your face.

The way she was wearing it now over one shoulder made her look young and vulnerable…and almost pretty. 'I don't care for it the way it is now…'

She put a self-conscious hand up towards her hair.

'Ok, I'll pin it back,' she whispered huskily.

'Good.' He was climbing into the car now. 'I'll see you tomorrow,' he told her curtly.

The powerful engine fired to life and she watched as he put it into gear and sped away from her towards the road.

She wondered where he was going—where he was spending the night.

But then, that was none of her business, she reminded herself crossly.

Victoria stood in front of the mirror and studied her reflection. The suit was boring, the shirt beneath it prim. But maybe Antonio wanted her to look businesslike so that she would be taken seriously as his wife.

Who knew what was going through his mind, or what this was all about.

Anyway, she had complied with his wishes, had even pinned her hair back into the chignon that he had requested. She bit down on the softness of her lower lip as she remembered how he'd told her he disliked her hair when it fell around her shoulders. The remark had hurt, but she couldn't understand why, because she didn't care what he thought of her, she reminded herself grimly.

She'd had to remember that fact a few times last night as she'd sat alone in the formal dining room being waited upon by Sarah. Had to remind herself that she'd rather have eaten alone than dine with a man who really didn't want her company. Yet a stark feeling of isolation had plagued her.

Crazy, given that she didn't want to be around Antonio anyway—and loneliness was something she was used to.

How was it she felt more lonely here than she did in her apartment when Nathan was in bed and she was eating a solitary supper?

Maybe it was just the fact that she missed her staff and friends in the restaurant. Maybe it was that she wasn't used to being waited on by someone and felt uncomfortable with that too. She had offered to eat in the kitchen, had asked if she could help with any chores that needed doing, but Sarah had looked appalled.

'It's not your place to work in a kitchen, Signora Cavelli!' she had said.

'But I've worked in a kitchen nearly all of my life,' she had told the woman quietly. 'And besides, I like cooking.'

The woman had pursed her lips and muttered something about it not being quite right or proper.

Whatever that meant. Victoria sighed. She couldn't pretend to be something she wasn't.

Today she had gone into the kitchen anyway and had made breakfast for herself and Nathan before the woman had realized she was in there.

'You really shouldn't be doing that,' Sarah had said when she'd walked in and found her. 'I'm supposed to be looking after you!'

'Well, I'm just not used to that!' Victoria had said honestly. 'And anyway, I was hoping if I spent some time with you in the kitchen I could pick up a few tips on authentic Italian cuisine while I was here.'

There had been a brief moment when she wasn't sure if the woman would just shoo her out anyway, but then the stern features had relaxed and she had shrugged. 'Every region of Italy has its own different authentic cuisine—which area were you interested in?'

It was strange but after that they seemed to get along quite well. They'd spent an amicable few hours glancing through recipe books and Victoria had felt more relaxed than she had in a long time. Certainly more relaxed than she felt now as she looked at the clock and saw that it was almost seven.

Antonio wasn't home yet but she supposed she should go downstairs to wait for him, so that he would know when he stepped into the house that she was ready to go. She glanced over at Nathan, who was sitting on the floor playing happily with some racing cars that he had found amidst the box of toys in his room. He looked cute in a pair of blue trousers and a white shirt, his dark hair brushed back from his face. Antonio's father couldn't help but be impressed with him, Victoria thought with a smile. Although she supposed she was biased.

'Come on, darling, we should go downstairs now.' She went over and held out her hand. Dutifully her son stood, although he brought the cars with him, sticking one in the pocket of his trousers and holding the other aloft to show her.

'Yes, lovely cars,' Victoria agreed with a smile and allowed him to take them with him. She supposed it wouldn't do any harm and she didn't want to risk him starting to cry, which happened sometimes when he was tired.

She'd given Nathan his dinner more than an hour ago. And under normal circumstances he would have been in bed by now, but due to jet lag he had slept for longer this afternoon and still seemed wide awake and in good humour now—but it was best to play things safe.

The clock was striking seven as Victoria walked downstairs and into the front lounge. Sarah appeared a few minutes later.

'Can I get you anything, *signora*?' she asked politely, whilst at the same time Victoria was aware that her gaze was moving over her with critical assessment.

'No, thank you, Sarah.' Victoria brushed a nervous hand down over her skirt.

'Very well…' The woman smiled at Nathan, who went running over to show her his cars. *'Bellissimo!'* The housekeeper's eyes warmed as she looked at the child. 'Adorable…' she told Victoria.

The approval surprised Victoria—as did the fact that her son didn't seem to be even slightly daunted by the formidable woman.

There was the sound of a car pulling up along the drive and Victoria's gaze moved towards the window.

'Ah, that will be the *signor*. I will tell him that you are waiting.' The housekeeper hurried out of the room and Victoria sat down on the sofa.

The house felt ominously silent, the only sound the ticking of the gold carriage clock on the mantelpiece.

Then suddenly she could hear footsteps on the parquet floor.

She looked up as Antonio appeared in the doorway and her heart seemed to constrict somewhere in her chest. He was wearing a dark cashmere suit that emphasized the powerful breadth of his shoulders. And the pinstripe shirt and plain grey silk tie complemented his Mediterranean dark good looks perfectly. By contrast he made her feel totally inadequate.

'Good evening, Victoria.' The cool Italian tones made her heart thud faster, as did the way his eyes swept with assessing intensity over her appearance. 'Are you ready to go?'

'Yes.' *Didn't she look ready?* Self-consciously she got to her feet. 'I've been waiting since seven as you requested,' she murmured, a note of defiance creeping into her voice.

'Good.' He merely looked amused and she noticed he didn't bother to apologize for keeping her waiting. His eyes lingered once more on the shapeless suit she was wearing, making her feel hot inside.

'You told me to wear it,' she found herself telling him defensively.

'Yes…and I was right. It's perfect.' His dark gaze met with hers. 'You are perfect.'

She frowned, knowing very well that she was not. For a second she remembered how her aunt used to mock her appearance. Remembered that even when she had made an effort to get contact lenses she had shrieked with laughter.

No, she knew very well that she was definitely not perfect. She looked away from him towards Nathan, who was standing quietly watching them, the red sports car still gripped in his little hand.

'I really think we should go,' she changed the subject stiffly. 'I don't want to be out late as it's well past Nathan's bedtime now.'

'Of course.' He noted the vulnerable way she looked away from him, as if desperate to escape. Obviously she didn't want his compliments—or didn't believe them. There was something poignant about her self-effacing attitude, something that made him…what…? Want to reassure her…protect her? He frowned, wondering where the hell his thoughts were going with this.

He was paying her well for her time—this was just a job.

He certainly wasn't going to start feeling…defensive towards her or about what he was doing.

'I wouldn't worry—we won't be out long. In fact, when we get there we might find dinner has to be postponed.'

The comment puzzled her. 'Why?'

'Because my father can be difficult,' Antonio muttered, his expression suddenly harsh.

'I see.' She frowned but didn't really understand. 'Do you think he will be angry that you've got married without inviting him to attend the ceremony?'

The thoughtful reasoning made him smile at her. 'No, I can safely say that won't be a factor he'll be concerned with.'

Antonio glanced down as Nathan toddled over to him, holding up his red racing car. 'So…what is that you have?' He crouched down so that he was at eye level with the child. 'I recognize that car.'

Nathan held it out closer for his inspection, with serious intent.

'Ah…' Antonio said with approval. 'Very fast, very sleek— one of the world's most desirable cars.'

Nathan looked suitably pleased and then giggled as he was lifted and swept up into powerful arms.

'Right, we shall go.'

Nathan seemed thrilled to be carried so high on Antonio's shoulder and he smiled at his mother as if to say, *Hey, look where I am.*

The whole situation felt slightly unreal, Victoria thought nervously. To a casual bystander they would probably have looked just like any ordinary family going out for the evening. But there was nothing ordinary about these circumstances.

Antonio had dismissed his driver for the evening and had his car waiting for them outside the front door.

'Do you have a different car for every day of the week?' she asked him in surprise.

'No, just every second day.' He cast an amused glance in her direction, but she wasn't looking at him now, because she was distracted by the fact that there was a child safety seat in the rear of the vehicle.

'Have you had that specially put in for Nathan?' she asked as she watched him fasten her son securely in.

'Well, it's not for my briefcase, if that's what you think, because I draw the line at that,' he joked, then glanced around at her more seriously. 'I thought as we are not using the limousine tonight that it would be best.'

'That's great, thanks! There are not many bachelors who would have thought ahead in that way.'

He grinned. 'Maybe you've just been out with a lot of thoughtless men.' He opened the passenger door for her and watched as she got in.

'Not really, but then I don't have much time to socialize,' she told him with a shrug.

He noticed that her skirt rode up a little as she got into the car, revealing shapely legs. Slamming the door closed, he walked around to get into the driver's seat.

'So when was the last time you went out on a date?' He couldn't resist the question as he flicked the powerful engine into life. And even in the darkness he could see that her skin was flushed with heat now.

'Are you referring to this evening as a date?' Swiftly she batted the question back. 'Because technically speaking, I don't think it is.'

Antonio smiled; he liked her shy yet fiery intelligent manner. It made him want to tease her, challenge her. 'Don't you? Well, correct me if I'm wrong, but technically I'd say a date can be any kind of a social rendezvous, can't it?' He shrugged.

'I don't think so.' She looked over at him pointedly. 'Not in the context you are using the word.'

'Really, and in what context was I using the word?' he asked humorously.

She felt herself getting hotter now. 'In a romantic way… and, well, you know it.'

'I didn't realize, Victoria, that you were such a stickler for detail.' He smiled at her and it did strange things to her senses, sent her heart fluttering somewhere down into her stomach and back up again.

She hated that he could have that effect on her. Because she knew all too well that he was just bantering with her, knew he wasn't remotely interested in when she had last gone out on a date. And if he knew the truth, that in reality she hadn't been out with a man in nearly three years, that her one reckless night with Nathan's father was the sole extent of her experience with men, he'd probably find that amusing, too.

Biting down on her lip she looked away from him. 'Yes, well, maybe I am…a stickler as you put it.' She tried to maintain an even tone. 'But I prefer the term *businesslike*. And after all, that is what you want from me, isn't it?'

'Yes, that's exactly what I want.' For a moment he looked across at her. The way she threw up barriers against him intrigued him. But it shouldn't, he reminded himself firmly. Because it meant that he had chosen wisely and he didn't have to worry that she would get carried away with this charade. 'At which moment I feel I should point out that you referred to me as a bachelor a few moments ago and, in technical terms, according to the gold band on your finger, I'm now your husband.'

'On paper,' she intercepted quickly.

'Indeed.' He flicked her a probing look. 'And in my father's presence.'

'Oh! I see!' She swallowed hard. She might have known what lay behind the reminder. 'Don't worry, I won't forget when we are with your father.'

Antonio gave a grim smile. 'Don't worry—I don't think there will be a chance for you to forget.'

What did that mean? Victoria wondered uneasily.

Silence fell between them. Antonio now seemed lost in his own private thoughts.

Victoria watched the ribbon of road as it twisted through the mountains. Beside them, the lake shimmered silver under the light of a full moon. And for a moment she allowed herself to savour the enchantment of the scenery. If she and Antonio really had been newlyweds on honeymoon this would have been so romantic…so perfect.

But nothing was further from the truth, she reminded herself as she glanced over at the stern expression on Antonio's face now.

They turned at some high gates and Antonio stopped and wound electric windows down to tap in a security code on a system attached to the pillar. The code allowed them access, and a few moments later the heavy iron gates opened and they swept through and down a long dark driveway.

The house came into view, its majestic towers and crenulated walls dramatically shadowed against the backdrop of mountain and lake.

It was beautiful yet somehow utterly sinister, Victoria reflected. Or maybe it just seemed that way because of the tension that was escalating inside of her.

They came to a halt beside a huge front door guarded on either side by stone lions that seemed to glare ferociously out into the night.

'Welcome to the homestead,' Antonio murmured, his tone mocking, then went on to say something in Italian that she couldn't understand.

'Sorry…what does that mean?' she asked him softly.

'It means…' He hesitated, as if searching for the exact translation. 'It means, welcome to the eye of the storm…'

She wanted to ask what that meant, but one look at the closed expression on Antonio's face and she didn't dare. Instead she got out of the car and busied herself, taking Nathan out from the backseat.

Antonio went ahead of her up to the front door and pressed the bell.

Despite the warmth of the evening Victoria felt cold as she followed him. She was glad of Nathan's warmth in her arms… because she was suddenly quite terrified.

CHAPTER EIGHT

VICTORIA had thought Antonio's home was grand but this was something else; this was more like a palace than a home. The marble-tiled floor in the massive entrance hall led through to a reception area lined with what looked like family portraits that dated back for generations. Behind that a majestic staircase branched into two separate directions, leading to a gallery above them. Victoria had the impression that if she wandered off alone in here she could easily have got lost. Not that she intended wandering anywhere alone. Even the butler who had answered the door to them was intimidating.

Antonio sent the man away and then led her along a dark panelled corridor.

He opened double doors into a drawing room that held a roaring log fire. Chandeliers sparkled over fine Persian rugs and dark wood furniture.

There was no sign of Antonio's father and they were completely alone. 'I'm starting to feel a bit nervous,' Victoria admitted softly.

'Don't worry about it—the old man just likes to make an entrance.'

Nathan was wriggling impatiently to get down from her arms and rather than struggle with him she allowed him to slip to the floor so that he could play with his cars.

'Do you want a drink?' Antonio moved to the sideboard and picked up one of the crystal decanters.

'No, thanks.' She was too much on edge to have a drink. 'Do you think your father will believe for one moment that our marriage is real?' Victoria asked him suddenly.

Antonio looked over at her. Up until today he'd have answered that he didn't particularly care what his father thought; in fact, he'd been looking forward to gloatingly telling the old man the truth, but a conversation with his lawyer earlier had put him off that idea. Roberto had counselled caution, had told him it was best to maintain the pretence of a relationship until the shares were actually transferred into his name. Antonio supposed he was right; he didn't want things to get messy. Anyway, it would be revenge enough to see his father's expression when he found out that Victoria already had a child and that child was no blood relative of his. 'I don't see why he shouldn't believe it,' he said nonchalantly. 'You're wearing my ring. We *are* married.'

'Yes, but…' She swallowed hard. 'I'm not your type, am I? And everyone knows it.'

Antonio frowned. 'To whom are you referring?'

'Well…everyone… Your accountant was very sceptical— I could see it in his expression.'

'Tom Roberts is just an employee who only thinks about money.'

'Well, then…there is your housekeeper. She knows full well—'

'Sarah isn't going to say anything.'

'She doesn't need to say anything, that's my point. People know that you have dated some of the world's most glamorous and perfect women. Your father will know that this marriage doesn't add up as soon as he sees me.'

Antonio's eyes narrowed on her for a moment and she blushed uncomfortably. 'I don't think so,' he said softly.

'I'm being realistic, Antonio.' She watched as he walked

across towards her. She had to be realistic—couldn't risk fooling herself for even a moment about this situation.

'Well, I think we can easily convince my father that we are a real couple.'

'You do?' He was standing very close to her now and she felt her emotions starting to dissolve into chaos as she looked up into the darkness of his eyes.

Was he just being kind? She couldn't think straight for a moment.

Something about the way he was looking at her was making her heart slam against her chest.

Vaguely she was aware of footsteps approaching along the hallway, but she couldn't drag her eyes away from Antonio.

He reached out and put his hands around her small waist and her heart missed several beats as surprise and consternation thundered through her. 'Antonio?'

Was he going to kiss her?

'Don't!' Her whispered plea was ignored as his head lowered towards hers.

She didn't want him to kiss her; she didn't want to know what it would feel like to be possessed by those lips, because she knew instinctively that it would be a dangerous kind of ecstasy. But too late—his mouth had captured hers.

She trembled violently under the onslaught to her senses, willing herself not to respond. But it felt so…so good. Pleasure flooded through her rigid body, unlocking her, heating her to boiling point. And before she knew what she was doing she was kissing him back.

Antonio felt a dart of surprise as he pulled her closer. He'd only been kissing her to prove a point to his father—had intended it just to be a mock display of passion. But… *hell*…this was intensely pleasurable.

He heard the door into the drawing room opening but he didn't let go of Victoria immediately, still he continued to kiss her. She felt so turned on! He could taste her need trembling from her lips…feel her hunger in every shiver of her slender body.

'Good evening, Antonio!' His father spoke in Italian and the cool words brought him sharply to his senses and he stepped back.

What was he thinking? Kissing Victoria wasn't supposed to be pleasurable! She was off-limits! This was strictly a business deal!

He looked down at her; she looked flustered…totally mortified. 'Are you OK?' he asked softly.

She didn't answer him…couldn't answer him.

Obviously the kiss had stunned her too. But there was no real harm done, Antonio told himself briskly. It was a moment of madness that had served its purpose. He glanced over her shoulder towards where his father was watching.

'You'll have to excuse us, Father,' he said quietly in Italian. 'But we are still on our honeymoon and can't quite drag ourselves away from each other.'

'You're…on honeymoon?' The man's voice was startled.

'Yes.' Antonio smiled and changed over to speaking in English. 'I'd like you to meet your new daughter-in-law.' He glanced down at Victoria. 'Turn around and say hello.'

She couldn't think straight…her mind was filled with the way Antonio had just made her feel and waves of confusion were flooding through her.

'Victoria.' His voice was firm, as were his eyes as he looked down at her.

Slowly she turned to do as he asked.

Victoria didn't think she would ever forget the look of surprise on the older man's face when he saw her.

'And you should also meet your grandson.' Antonio switched back to speaking in Italian again as he indicated Nathan, who was sitting quietly on the floor beside them playing with his cars. 'Not a blood relative, I'm afraid—but some things are just not meant to be.'

Clearly Luc Cavelli hadn't noticed Nathan until that moment. Victoria watched the man's expression turn from dismay and shock to outright fury.

She didn't understand anything of what was being said now but she knew from the grim tone in both of the men's voices that this was not a pleasant exchange, and she certainly didn't have to be fluent in Italian to know that Antonio's father was very displeased with his son's choice of wife.

As if sensing the tension in the air Nathan suddenly started to cry. 'There, darling, don't worry.' Victoria bent down and picked him up, cradling him close. She tried to sound reassuring but in reality she was shaking inside. The confusion she felt over Antonio's kiss and now his father's unwelcoming attitude were all just too much to bear.

Then suddenly without a word Antonio's father turned around and stormed out, slamming the doors behind him with an almighty bang.

The noise made Nathan stop crying and he looked around to see what had happened.

Then there was silence and Antonio smiled. 'That went well, I thought.'

'Excuse me?' She stared at him as if he were quite mad. 'It went terribly! Obviously he hates me…and…what the hell was that kiss all about?' Despite her best efforts to control her emotions, her voice wobbled precariously.

Antonio's eyes narrowed on the pallor of her skin. 'You know what the kiss was about,' he told her coolly. 'I thought I made it clear—it was about ensuring my father took our marriage seriously.'

Of course it was, she realized dully. A man like Antonio would never have any real feeling for someone like her.

Fierce pain thundered through her as she remembered how passionately she had responded. What a fool she was…

'You had no right to touch me like that!' Her voice trembled with sudden anger.

'Let's not get this out of proportion, Victoria. You and I have a business deal, that's all. And I told you I expected you to play your part.'

The coolness of his reply made the pain and anger inside of her intensify. 'But I didn't agree to kiss you!' she cut across him fiercely.

'Once our lips met I thought you were okay about it.' He looked at her pointedly. 'You didn't exactly try to pull away…did you?'

She tried to angle her chin up. But her distress was palpable. And a sudden sharp feeling stabbed through Antonio as his eyes raked over her.

She looked so vulnerable…so hurt. And for a moment it was as if he were seeing her for the first time, taking in everything about her. The tender way she held the child, the look in her eyes… The flush of colour over her high cheekbones…the way she was pretending not to have enjoyed the kiss—when in reality she most definitely had.

He muttered something in Italian, something that sounded fiercely angry.

'Do you think you could speak in English…please?' she asked him quietly.

He hesitated and then shook his head. 'Let's go home, Victoria.'

Antonio lay in bed staring up into the darkness. He had achieved exactly what he had set out to achieve and the shares in Cavelli Enterprises were now as good as his.

No doubt his father would be rallying his lawyers at first light but there was nothing they would be able to do—the old man had stitched himself up into a corner and Antonio had ensured there was no way out for him.

He should have felt jubilant. After all, he had spent the past ten years of his life dedicating himself to building the company up to where it was today. If he'd just walked away instead of challenging his father like this, everything would have been blown apart. And OK, he could have just stepped away into the life raft of his other company, Lancier, but how comfortable would he have felt with that as he watched the train wreck of Cavelli? Shares would have crashed, jobs would have been lost—and all because his father hadn't got his own way. But of course his father wouldn't see it like that; all he cared about was himself.

Grimly Antonio stared into the darkness. A major catastrophe had been averted just by a simple marriage of convenience, so why didn't he feel euphoric?

Why did he keep seeing Victoria's stricken face as she'd stood before him in his father's house? Why did he feel angry with himself for even bringing her there?

She was gaining a lot from this situation, he reminded himself angrily for the billionth time—a fabulous new restaurant, a lovely new home. What the hell was wrong with him?

As for that kiss…it *had* just been for show and she should have understood that. After all, she'd been the one to point out that Luc might question the validity of their marriage. A little bit of a smokescreen had been necessary. He just wished he hadn't enjoyed it quite so much. Victoria was for business only.

Impatiently he threw the covers back and got up from the bed. Dawn was breaking outside; he'd get an early start in at the office and forget this nonsense.

A little while later, showered and dressed ready for work, Antonio made his way downstairs. He'd planned to head straight out to his car, but a quick glance at his watch made him decide to have a coffee first.

It was a shock to find Victoria already in the kitchen. She had her back to him and she was staring out of the window, lost in thought.

What was she thinking about? he wondered.

He put his briefcase down onto the sideboard and she spun around in surprise.

'You startled me! I didn't realize anyone would be up at this hour!'

'Yes…so I see.' His eyes drifted lazily over her slender form.

She was wearing the long blue satin dressing gown that he'd seen on her during their flight. It didn't cling, just gently skimmed her curves, and her dark hair was loose and tumbled around her shoulders in glossy perfusion.

She looked so…different, he thought objectively. The blue of the dressing gown brought out the vivid green of her eyes. And her hair really was quite beautiful; it glistened under the overhead kitchen lights, the colour of rich chestnut.

Self-consciously she put a hand up to her hair and he remembered how he'd told her that he didn't like it loose.

Impatient with himself he transferred his attention towards his briefcase and snapped it open. He wasn't interested in Victoria and he didn't want to give her the impression that he was.

'I thought I'd get an early start and beat the traffic going into Verona this morning,' he told her idly. 'What's your excuse?'

For a moment she hesitated before answering honestly, 'I couldn't sleep.'

He glanced back at her. 'You're probably still jet lagged— I know I am.'

'Probably.'

As their eyes connected, memories from the night before flooded painfully through her. That kiss and subsequent scene at his father's house, the tense angry atmosphere that had accompanied their journey home—all had haunted her throughout the night, *especially the kiss*.

She still didn't understand what had happened to her when their lips had met; it was as if she had completely lost her mind. The only thing she did know was that it was best forgotten, she told herself angrily. As was the fact that his father had hated her and had obviously had other ideas for whom he wanted for his son's wife.

She didn't care, she told herself fiercely.

Hastily she looked away from him. 'I'll get out of your way.'

'No need.' He glanced over at the coffee pot on the stove. 'In fact, you may as well make yourself useful and pour me a coffee whilst you're here.'

Victoria frowned. She didn't want to make herself useful; she wanted to escape to the privacy of her own room. She needed to get dressed; she felt completely at a disadvantage walking around like this. Especially as he looked his usual suave sophisticated self.

But his tone wasn't one to argue with.

Antonio moved towards the table and flicked through some correspondence that he needed to deal with when he got into work.

But out of the corner of his eye he found himself watching her as she moved around the kitchen.

'There.' She put the steaming mug of coffee down onto the table for him next to a jug of cream and sugar. 'Now, if you'll excuse me I'll go and get dressed.'

Her cool manner irritated him. And impulsively he reached out and caught hold of her arm before she could move past him. 'No, I don't think I will excuse you,' he grated huskily.

Immediately he saw the colour flow up into her cheekbones like a rose-washed tide.

He liked the way her skin flushed, liked her fire laced with her fragility…and that in turn bothered him.

Frowning, he let go of her. 'Before you go rushing off, there are a few engagements we need to discuss.'

'Engagements?' She looked at him numbly. All she wanted to do was escape. What the hell was he talking about? 'What kind of engagements?'

'Dinner engagements—you know the kind of thing. Mostly business functions, but I'll need you to attend them with me.'

'Why?' She stared up at him, horrified by the suggestion, and he smiled.

'Because that's the kind of thing wives do. And for the time being as you *are* my wife, Victoria, your presence will be expected.' He tossed down a few of the invitations that he had just opened.

With trepidation she reached and picked one of the gold-embossed cards up. The invitation was in Italian, but judging by the beautifully drawn illustration of a man and woman, the dress code was formal black tie. 'This is for tomorrow evening!' she noticed in consternation. 'And it's in Venice!'

'Yes, I've already accepted that one a few weeks ago.' Antonio told her. 'It's for a charity ball, and as I'm one of the main benefactors and giving a speech I have to attend.'

'But surely you don't need me there?' She looked up at him almost pleadingly. 'I mean, you must go to these functions on your own all the time.'

'No, I usually have a partner with me.' He flicked her a sardonic look and her skin burnt with embarrassment.

What was she thinking! Of course Antonio Cavelli probably always had a glamorous woman on his arm.

'And I've accepted the invitation plus one,' he continued. 'So you will have to come with me.'

'I can't! I've no one to look after Nathan—'

'Sarah will look after him.'

She shook her head. 'You could just make my apologies,' she told him gruffly. 'You could say that I'm ill or something!'

He reached out and tipped her chin upwards so that she was forced to look at him. 'But you're not ill, are you?' he said softly. 'So what are you so afraid of, Victoria?'

The question and the touch of his hand made her skin burn fiercely.

He was standing far too close to her. She could see the hazel flecks in the darkness of his eyes—eyes that were so...so sexy. And she noticed suddenly how his gaze had moved towards her lips.

Hastily she wrenched herself away from him. *She was*

afraid of allowing herself to even think about that kiss again! Of having her heart broken...of making a fool of herself with someone who was far beyond her reach!

'I just don't want to go!' she told him fiercely. 'And I don't remember agreeing to such a thing. You didn't tell me that our...business arrangement was going to include things like this!'

'I'm telling you now,' he replied calmly.

'You'll just have to take someone else!' she suggested in desperation.

'Like a girlfriend?' His eyes narrowed on her and there was a tense silence. 'I am not my father, Victoria. That is out of the question.'

The angry words swirled uncomfortably between them and she looked away. It was crazy but there was a little place in her heart that was relieved he had turned down that suggestion. And that made her cross with herself. He was not hers, and he never would be. Once this was all over and he filed for divorce or an *annulment* she would never see him again. And he would be back to dating whoever he wanted.

He closed his briefcase and reached for his coffee. 'Now run along and get dressed,' he told her firmly. 'I'll take you into Verona with me so you can buy yourself some new clothes.'

She felt totally panic-stricken now. 'But I have Nathan to see to and he's still asleep.'

'Sarah will look after him. She'll be down in a moment and I'll clear it with her.' He held up a hand before she could say anything. 'I'd trust Sarah with my life,' he told her succinctly. 'She's the most capable person I know—now stop arguing with me and do as you are told.'

She wanted to argue some more but she was fast running out of reasons to give him...well, reasons she could voice anyway...

All she knew was that spending too much time with Antonio was a dangerous mistake. She couldn't allow herself to get too close.

But she could hardly tell him that!

So after a moment's hesitation Victoria headed for the door. It seemed she had no alternative but go along with this charade for now.

Half an hour later they were driving down beside the crystal clear waters of Lake Garda and then through lush mountainous scenery laced with vineyards and olive groves.

Antonio had the top down on his red sports car and the warmth of the autumn morning was gentle against her skin.

She wished she could relax. There really was nothing to worry about, she told herself sternly. Nathan had seemed happily contented in Sarah's arms when they left. And Sarah had been more than willing to look after him. Had volunteered her babysitting services quite happily for anytime they wanted to go out.

Victoria wished she hadn't done that.

'Is this your first visit to Italy?' Antonio broke the silence suddenly.

She nodded. 'When I was younger and lived in England, my parents never had the money for holidays. That's not to say they weren't happy,' she added hastily, 'because they were. They loved each other very much.'

'And what about you—were you happy?'

The question caught her by surprise. 'Yes, when they were together I was. We used to go for days out to Brighton.' She smiled. 'I remember Dad buying me ice cream, and letting me have a ride at the funfair.'

'You miss him.'

'Yes, I suppose I still do. Everything sort of fell apart when he died. Mum missed him so much. He was the love of her life.' She blushed suddenly. 'That's if you believe in that sort of thing.'

'Not really.' Antonio smiled. 'Although I know I should— we Italians have a reputation for being romantics, so…' He shrugged. 'I'm letting the side down, but there it is.'

'You're a realist.'

'Something like that.'

'Me too.' It felt good telling him that...*especially after that kiss last night.*

He smiled and put the car into top gear and they roared over the lanes and hills, until in the distance below the fields of poppies and vines she could see the city of Verona shimmering in the sunshine.

'It looks so beautiful,' she murmured.

'And forever linked with love and romance.' Antonio told her. 'There is a house at the heart of the city known as the *Casa di Giulietta*, which is reputed to be the house of Juliet—as in Romeo and Juliet. Apparently the building was once home to the Cappello family and folklore has it that Shakespeare drew his inspiration from them. The famous balcony is probably one of the most popular tourist attractions in this town.'

'I'll have to take a look.'

'Indeed.' His dark eyes glinted with amusement. 'Not that you are a romantic or anything.'

'No.' She frowned, wondering if he was teasing her now. 'Certainly not.'

Silence fell between them again; he glanced over and saw the rapt expression on her face as they drove into the city. 'It's a beautiful city, isn't it?' he said softly.

'Yes, I didn't expect it to be so lovely, and it feels so Mediterranean with the surrounding hills covered in olive groves and vineyards.'

He nodded. 'The hills are home to the Valpolicella wine region and the famous Amarone wine of Veneto.'

'I don't think I've tried the Amarone wine,' she said with a frown.

He looked at her with mock horror. 'We will have to put that right over lunch.'

'No, I can't stay to have lunch. I shall have to get back home to Nathan before then!' she told him hastily. 'I can't leave him with Sarah for too long!'

'Sarah has had four children of her own and she has six grandchildren, Victoria. I think she is more than capable of looking after one little boy for the day.'

She knew he was right, knew she could trust Sarah. But the thought of having lunch with Antonio was ringing alarm bells inside of her.

'Has anyone ever told you that you are very bossy?' she muttered, not knowing what else to say.

'No. Has anyone ever told you that you are very stubborn?' he countered with a teasing glance.

She shook her head but couldn't help but smile and capitulate. 'You always have the last word, don't you?'

'Absolutely.'

They were driving around beside what looked like an old Roman arena now. The place looked fascinating. Opposite there was a wide road lined with sophisticated pavement cafés and restaurants.

'Unfortunately I have to go straight into the office,' Antonio continued. 'But after you've done your shopping we can meet back here.'

She felt tremendously relieved that he wasn't going to accompany her into shops. That would have been too horrendously embarrassing.

As he turned the car down a side street, he pointed out to her where she should walk and where they would meet, and then he drove across and down into an underground private car park that bore the gold emblem of Cavelli Enterprises.

'This is my company headquarters,' he told her as he parked in the private space that bore his name. 'Any problems and you can come back here to find me. Just take the lift up to my office on the top floor.' He nodded towards a doorway opposite. 'Tell the security guard that you are my wife and he'll show you the way.'

Tell the security guard that you are my wife... For some

reason the words played tantalizingly through her mind, before she swiftly dismissed them. She wasn't his wife…not in any real or meaningful way.

'I won't have a problem,' she told him quickly.

'Good.' He reached into his jacket pocket and took out his wallet. 'But maybe you better take my business card anyway with my telephone number…oh, and your credit card, of course.' He pulled a gold card out. 'I've set up an account for you in your married name.'

She looked at the card, suddenly completely stricken. She had no intention of being beholden to him in that way! 'I can buy my own clothes!'

'Victoria how much cash have you got on you?'

She glared at him furiously. 'I have enough to buy a dress.'

'You also need to buy accessories and a few cocktail dresses for the other engagements coming up. And you don't want to be skimping on quality.'

He thought she would be buying bargain basement clothes. She felt herself heat up with embarrassment. Because in all honesty she probably would—she didn't have enough money to buy the kind of designer quality he was talking about. But she still wasn't going to take his money; she had her pride! 'It's OK…I'll manage!'

He shook his head. 'I've never come across a woman like you! Never met a woman who seemed insulted by my offering to buy her a dress…and the fact that we are married makes it all the more bizarre!'

'But…it's not a real marriage.' She looked away from him out at the car park. 'So let's not get carried away with this.'

'No…let's not.' For a second there was silence, and she could feel the tension between them twisting in the air. 'But you still have a part to play, Victoria.'

She looked around at him. 'Are you worried that I'm going to ruin your reputation for only being seen with the world's most beautiful and well-dressed women?'

'No, don't be absurd!' His eyes held with hers. 'And I'm sure you will look lovely no matter what you choose to wear.'

'Liar…' The whispered word trembled in the air between them.

Victoria felt hot inside at the way his gaze travelled down over the grey suit she was wearing.

There was nothing wrong with it, he thought drily—it was just rather staid…and it hid any curves she had. His eyes lingered on the way the buttons of her white blouse were fastened up almost to her chin and he smiled.

'Sometimes I get the feeling that you like to hide yourself away…but as a matter of fact your prim sense of style is starting to grow on me.'

Her skin was awash with colour now. How patronizing could you get! How dare he say something like that to her!

'I don't hide myself away! I'll have you know that I dress in a businesslike way for businesslike occasions! Our so-called wedding day being one of them!'

'And that's fine.' He shrugged. 'But you can't wear a businesslike suit to a Venetian ball, can you?' He reached out and took hold of her hand and the touch of his skin against hers made her tremble inside.

'But it does mean that you can accept this in the same businesslike spirit with which I am offering it.' Before she realized what he was doing he had placed the card into her hand and was curling her fingers over it with firm insistence. 'Call it my investment in the commodities market,' he grated sardonically.

'Ha, ha, very funny.' Her voice felt a little raw.

'You've got three hours to buy about three outfits—cocktail dresses, and a suitable dress for the ball. Now go.'

CHAPTER NINE

Just who did Antonio Cavelli think he was? Victoria asked herself angrily as she strode along the pedestrian Via Mazzini shopping area.

How dare he talk to her like that!

And how dare he accuse her of hiding herself away! She wasn't hiding away from anything or anyone; she dressed to please herself, not to please any man, and certainly not to try and please him!

Just because she wasn't swooning every time he looked at her, like all the other women he met, he obviously thought there was something wrong with her! The man was arrogant and conceited beyond words....

Realizing suddenly that she was marching past all of the shops without even glancing in the windows she came to an abrupt halt. She needed to calm down and focus.

She needed to buy three good outfits and show Antonio that she did know a thing or two about fashion despite his patronizing opinion!

The man had a damn nerve.

She went across to the window opposite and looked in. It was a designer shop; the clothes were exquisite and probably very expensive because there didn't appear to be a price on anything. One maxi dress in particular caught her eye; it was a halter neck. The material was the softest shimmering silk in a shade of turquoise shot through with midnight blue.

For a long moment she stood admiring it, then she frowned at herself. Who was she kidding—she'd look hideous in that dress; it would be far too clingy and the neckline was far too revealing for her!

Impatiently she moved on to the next shop. The Italian styles were beautiful, the leather the most superb quality, the shoes...sexy beyond belief. It felt slightly surreal wandering around these sophisticated boutiques, looking at clothes that would normally have been not only out of her price bracket but also out of her lifestyle bracket back home.

She didn't go anywhere to warrant them; most of her evenings were either spent working, or in with Nathan. And even as the proud owner of a stylish new restaurant, the clothes she was looking at here would still not be sensible. She was too hands-on; more often than not she worked in the kitchen, rather than front of house.

Frowning, she suddenly realized that she was being her usual practical self.

And that was almost certainly what Antonio was expecting. He probably thought she wouldn't have a clue what to buy. Was doubtless expecting her to look bad no matter what! What was it he had said so condescendingly? *'Your prim sense of style is starting to grow on me.'*

She bit down on her lip. How dare he mock her like that!

A sales assistant came over and spoke to her in Italian, bringing her out of her reverie.

'I'm sorry, I don't speak Italian...'

The woman smiled politely. 'Would you like to try that dress on?' she asked in beautifully accented English. 'Can I be of any assistance?'

Victoria looked down at the provocative little dress she had in her hand.

She didn't have to be practical today, she reminded

herself fiercely—she was in Italy shopping for outfits for exclusive parties and summer balls. And the gold card that Antonio had insisted she have was still burning a hole in her purse.

For once in her life she could afford to be frivolous.

She was fifteen minutes late. Antonio sat in the sunshine and perused the menu lazily. He wasn't used to being kept waiting. Women were usually eagerly waiting for him. He'd give her another five minutes, then he'd phone to see if she'd got lost.

He had to get back to work in just under an hour—there was a mountain of paperwork that needed sorting out after his trip to Australia. In reality he shouldn't have taken time off for lunch today—he couldn't quite work out why he had. Maybe because he'd felt sympathy for Victoria—it couldn't be easy for her coming here and not speaking the language, and being dragged to functions she really didn't want to attend. Lord alone knew what she was buying to wear for their evening out tomorrow! He smiled to himself. Maybe he should have got one of his women friends to go shopping with her.

The waiter appeared at his table and he ordered a bottle of Amarone and two glasses. Then as he was left alone again, he watched the people walking by on the pavement. There was a sleepy heat to the afternoon—not much traffic on the road now, just a few horse-drawn carriages giving tourists a ride around the town.

The gentle murmur of Italian voices from the other diners in the restaurant was relaxing, the smell of roasted coffee floated in the air.

A beautiful woman smiled provocatively as she walked past him to get a table. But Antonio hardly registered her; his gaze flicked impatiently to his watch again.

Then he saw Victoria turning around the corner heading towards him. She was laden down with bags, but she was walking with a breezy confidence that made him smile. She seemed young and carefree, her head held high. He hadn't seen her look like that before.

She noticed him as she got closer and she smiled. 'Sorry I'm late.'

'That's OK, I'll forgive you.' He stood politely and waited for her to take the chair opposite him before reclaiming his seat.

He was so urbane, so lazily attractive, that she could feel her heart speeding up a little. Desperately she tried to look unfazed, as if she were used to meeting sharp-suited handsome Italian men for lunch.

'I take it your shopping trip was successful, judging by all those bags?' he enquired.

'Yes, it was…thank you.' She reached for the glass of wine that he had poured for her. 'It was great.'

'It's a good city for shopping,' he acknowledged.

'Yes, a fabulous city. And I've decided that I adore Italy,' she added impulsively. 'Everything is so stylish here…even the pavements!'

Her enthusiasm was infectious and he laughed. 'Some are made from the local marble, Rosa Verona.'

'Very pleasing to the eye.' She smiled at him. It was strange but she felt on a high after her shopping spree and more relaxed than she could remember in a long time.

'I'm glad you are so enamoured.' He regarded her with a steady dark gaze. 'So…does this mean that despite your reservations about coming to Italy, it won't be such a chore for you to live here for a while…hmm?'

The question made her pause. 'No, it won't be a chore,' she told him honestly. 'I'm sure I could be more than happy to live here…for a while.' She added the proviso just as he had, conscious that whatever her feelings, her time here would only ever be fleeting

Their eyes held for a moment and then she looked swiftly away.

'The arena looks interesting.' She glanced across the road towards the large Roman amphitheatre.

'Yes, it's about two thousand years old and is like the one in Rome only smaller and more complete. Nowadays, however, instead of gladiators battling we have opera festivals.' He leaned back in his chair. 'Some of the world's leading artists have sung there. It's a great venue and one of the largest open-air stages in the world.'

'It must be a fabulous experience to attend.'

'It is. But you have the world-famous opera house in Sydney that is a great venue also.'

'I'm sure it is.'

'You haven't been?'

'Well...I've stood on the steps outside...but I don't think that counts, does it?' She smiled shyly. 'Maybe when I go back I'll have a night out there.' Awkwardly she reached for her wine and took a sip. Part of her didn't want to think about going home and the other part of her was telling her to think of nothing else. 'Is this the famous Amarone that you were telling me about?' She found herself changing the subject swiftly. 'It's very good. I'll have to look into stocking it at the restaurant.'

'Definitely not a wine to be overlooked,' he agreed easily. 'How are things going with the restaurant, by the way? I didn't have time to look in on it before we left Sydney.'

'Things are running pretty much to schedule. The kitchen units have been stripped and waxed, the new carpets and wood flooring are down. I'm just waiting for delivery now of the new tables and chairs that I've ordered. Oh, and Claire is waiting for me to make a decision on work tops.' She smiled. 'I have several brochures to look through.'

'If you want to phone her, or use the computer in my office at home, then feel free.'

'Thanks, that would be a help.'

'I've set up a bank account for you here and paid an allowance which should help with your expenses. Also you must use that card I gave you for anything you need.'

The casual words made her body heat up in consternation. 'We've had this conversation earlier! I don't feel comfortable with you bankrolling me—'

'As you say, we've had the conversation.' He looked at her pointedly. 'There is no point arguing with me, Victoria.'

Antonio signalled for the waiter to come over. 'Now we should order,' he told her. 'Regretfully, I haven't got much time as I have to get back to work.'

Victoria picked up the menu and tried to switch off the cold subject of money. 'What would you recommend?' she asked, turning her attention to the food.

'The *bigoli* here is good. It's a kind of large spaghetti. Also the *gnocchi*.'

She read through his suggestions and then ordered the *bigoli* with white sea bream to follow.

As the waiter retreated she continued to study the menu with interest for several moments. And Antonio allowed his gaze to travel over her.

A few of the buttons on her blouse hadn't been fastened up. She'd probably been in a rush to get dressed again after trying clothes on. He could see the top of her white lacy bra. It was somehow very sexy, which he found somewhat curious because she wasn't dressed in any way provocatively. In fact, of all the women he had ever dined with she was probably the most covered up.

The last woman he'd taken out had been wearing a dress with a plunging neckline that had left nothing to the imagination—and he hadn't found that nearly as alluring as that tantalizing piece of lace right now.

Very strange, he thought deprecatingly, his eyes moving higher.

She'd caught the sun a little today; her skin looked radiant.

And her hair had worked its way to the side and lay over her shoulder in a thick glossy plait.

She looked up and caught him watching her, caught the gleam of male interest in his eye. Then as he smiled she looked away in confusion. She must have been mistaken; there was no way Antonio would be looking at her with any real interest. He'd made it more than clear that this was business and she just wasn't his type.

'The…the menu is very interesting,' she told him, trying to focus on something else.

'Is it?' He sounded lazily amused by the observation.

'Yes…the selection of dishes are…' She trailed away as she noticed how one of his eyebrows lifted. 'Sorry, I can get a bit carried away with food issues, it's an—'

'Occupational hazard.' He finished the words for her with a smile. 'Don't worry, we Italians are also very passionate about our food.'

'I've heard that you Italians are very passionate about a lot of things,' she said with a laugh.

'Have you now?' There was teasing warmth in his eyes that made her blush.

'Yes, I believe as a nation you are very passionate about football.'

'We certainly are.' He smiled at her. 'Amongst other things…'

The waiter brought some cold antipasto and put it in the centre of the table, along with some freshly baked bread. There was prosciutto ham and luscious green and black olives, and some roasted vegetables with goat's cheese.

'Now, if you are interested in new dishes for your restaurant you should try the chef's special twist on *giardinara*,' Antonio told her, indicating the small serving of food that she had been wondering about.

'What is it?' She leaned forward with interest.

'Fresh vegetables in a tart marinade. Try a little.' He cut a piece of the warm bread and spooned some of the dish on, then held it out to her.

She was going to take it from him but he placed the bite-size portion to her lips. There was something very intimate about the gesture and it made her heart speed up, made her breathing slow down—it was the weirdest feeling.

'What do you think?' he asked with a smile.

'Delicious.'

'Food should be like life, don't you think? It should excite the senses…'

Her eyes met with his.

'You blush beautifully, do you know that?' he asked softly.

For a moment she felt the warmth of his eyes almost like the sun beating down on them. With difficulty she gathered herself together. 'I know that you are a flirt, Antonio! But I suppose it comes naturally to Italians, like breathing?'

He laughed. 'For a woman who has never been to Italy you come to the table with a lot of preconceived ideas.'

'Most of them are right though, aren't they?' she countered, angling her chin up.

'Some of them are right,' he corrected her with a smile. 'I'll leave you to discover which in your own time.'

She tried not to like him—she tried really hard not to surrender to the magnetic personality, the dark sexy eyes—but the warmth of the day and the mellow flow of the conversation started to invade her senses.

By the time they had finished their main courses and the waiter stopped by their table to ask if they wanted anything else, she realized that they had been talking about nothing in particular with complete enjoyment for the past hour.

Antonio glanced at his watch. 'I will have to be getting back, I'm afraid.'

'Yes…me too, otherwise Nathan will be wondering where I am.'

Antonio asked the waiter for the bill and they were left alone again.

'I'll get my chauffeur to pick you up and take you home,' Antonio told her briskly.

'There's no need—isn't there a bus or taxi or something?'

He laughed. 'Why would the wife of a multimillionaire take the bus home?' There was no conceit about the statement, just a teasing quality that made her shrug awkwardly.

'Because she *likes* to be independent?'

He smiled. 'Sorry! You will have to put up with Alberto,' he said as he flipped open his phone and made a swift call in Italian. 'The car will be here in five minutes.'

She shrugged—what else could she do? 'Thank you.'

For a moment as she looked at him across the table she didn't want the afternoon to end; she wanted it to go on and on...

A woman stopping by the table interrupted them and they both looked up.

'Elizabetta!' Antonio got easily to his feet and kissed the attractive brunette on both cheeks and they talked animatedly for a few moments in Italian before Antonio switched to English to introduce Victoria.

The woman smiled politely at her. 'I don't think we have met before,' she said in perfect English.

She was stunning, Victoria thought, probably about thirty with long loose curls around a perfectly made-up face. She was wearing a figure-hugging black dress with a wide patent-leather belt clinching it to her small waist.

'Victoria has just come back with me from Australia,' Antonio answered casually. 'We were married a few days ago.'

There was a moment's startled silence. 'You've got married!'

To say the woman looked flabbergasted was putting it mildly. She glanced back at Antonio as if half expecting him to tell her he was only joking.

'I don't believe it! The man who swore he would never marry!'

She was in love with him, Victoria realized suddenly. She could see it in the hurt expression of her dark eyes as she looked up at him.

'It was a whirlwind decision,' Antonio said with a shrug.

The woman nodded and seemed to pull herself together. 'Well, congratulations.' She looked over at Victoria again. 'I hope you will both be very happy.'

'Thank you.' Victoria smiled uncomfortably.

'I better go, or I shall be late back to work.' Elizabetta looked at Antonio again.

'It was nice to see you,' she said softly. 'I can't believe you are married! One of the world's most eligible bachelors bites the dust—finally.'

He laughed at that.

As she walked away from them, Victoria looked across at Antonio. 'She seems lovely.'

'Yes. She works for an advertising agency that I use from time to time.'

'And she's obviously an ex-girlfriend?'

Antonio looked at her wryly and she found herself heating up. 'Not that it is any of my business,' she murmured uncomfortably.

'We went out a few times over a year ago. But it was never serious,' he said with a shrug.

She wanted to say, *It was never serious on* your *part.* But she didn't dare voice the words. It was none of her concern how many women's hearts he had broken, she told herself sternly, just as long as she was never one of them.

The limousine drew up at the curb and Antonio picked up her shopping bags and walked with her to the car to hand them over to the driver.

'I'll see you tomorrow evening in Venice,' he told her.

'You're not coming home tonight?'

He shook his head. 'No, I'll be working late so I may as well stay at my apartment here in town.'

'Yes, of course.' She nodded and tried to look as if she didn't care. She had no right to care, and more than that, she didn't want to care, she reminded herself angrily. But as she looked up at him she felt an almost unbearable twist of emotion curling inside of her.

'So…I'm…to meet you in Venice?' she clarified huskily.

'Yes, it's a bit of a trek, so I'll send the helicopter for you. That's if it doesn't offend your independent sensibilities?'

'If it did you wouldn't pay any attention,' she countered, and he smiled.

'I might,' he said softly. 'Anyway, we'll stay overnight at the Cavelli hotel on the Grand Canal.'

'Overnight!' Victoria frowned. 'I can't possibly leave Nathan overnight!'

'Relax—I'm not suggesting you leave him. Sarah will come with you and babysit. She'll enjoy an evening at the Cavelli.'

'But—'

'I have to go, Victoria,' he cut across her firmly and nodded at the driver to open the rear passenger door for her. 'So I'll see you in Venice.'

CHAPTER TEN

THE helicopter arrived a little after four-thirty in the afternoon. And as it smoothly lowered down onto the lawn at the front of the house, the noise from the blades echoed off the surrounding mountains in a cacophony of sound.

'Look, Nathan, a helicopter.' Victoria stood at the windows in her bedroom and lifted her son up so that he could look out. 'Aren't you a lucky boy going for a ride in one of those?'

She had to smile at the child's wide-eyed enthusiasm. Nothing really fazed Nathan. She wished she could say the same about herself.

Part of her was so excited about this trip—she'd always wanted to go to Venice, and the thought of attending a ball with Antonio was a little dreamlike. But then she remembered her circumstances and she didn't dare allow herself to be excited. The way she'd felt when Antonio had made it clear to her that he wouldn't be returning home last night was still playing on her mind. That sharp unexplainable little ache had stayed with her on the journey back to his house and had continued to torment her ever since. And it terrified her.

Irritated with herself she put her son down and went to fasten up the straps on the overnight bag that Sarah had found for her to use. She wasn't going to dwell on her response to Antonio, because it didn't mean anything…just as their kiss had meant nothing, she told herself sternly. OK, she'd enjoyed a relaxing lunch with a handsome man...and maybe Antonio had made her aware of herself as a woman for the first time in years, made her realize that deep down she was a little bit lonely.

But that was all there was to it.

There was a knock on the door and Sarah put her head around to tell her it was time to go.

'OK, won't be a moment.' She smiled at the housekeeper. She didn't know why she had ever thought the woman was a dragon, because she had been so very wrong!

Sarah had helped her a lot today. Had offered to take care of Nathan whilst she'd had her hair done, and then had assisted her with her packing. It was on her advice that Victoria was going to change into her evening dress once they got to the hotel. Apparently there would be plenty of time, and it would mean she could meet Antonio feeling refreshed and relaxed.

Victoria wasn't sure about that last bit; her nerves jangled a bit every time she thought about seeing Antonio tonight. But she had taken Sarah's advice and was travelling in a casual little skirt and top that she'd purchased on impulse yesterday.

She lifted Nathan up and hugged him. 'OK, honey...we are off on our adventure,' she said softly.

Victoria would never forget that magical journey to Venice. She was treated first to a bird's-eye view of the magnificent Lake Garda in all its spectacular glory; the dramatic mountain scenery and little villages were awe inspiring. The ferries cutting across the vivid blue of the water looked like toy ships in a make-believe land. Then away over the mountains and the vineyards they swept out towards the sea, approaching Venice as the sun started to set and light the sky with vivid apricot flames.

The surreal colour reflected off the water by the Rialto where gondolas plied their trades, and then dazzled over the golden rooftops and spires of the city.

Sarah pointed out the Cavelli hotel, which was built in the Renaissance style overlooking the Grand Canal. The domes at either side and the grand columns and archways gave it a regal air of sophistication. They swept around and over the large rooftop terrace to the helipad at one side. And Nathan clapped in delight as they came slowly down to land.

Victoria caught Sarah's eye and they both smiled. 'He'll sleep tonight after all this excitement,' Sarah said with a laugh.

The blades whirled to a halt and a member of staff walked across the terrace to open the doors and welcome them.

Victoria felt like a VIP as she stepped out into the evening air. Attentive staff rushed to take their luggage and the manager of the hotel was waiting to personally greet her and to congratulate her most sincerely on her marriage.

'We have prepared the main suite for you, Signora Cavelli, just as your husband instructed,' he said, turning to lead the way across the terrace by an Olympic-size swimming pool and through some French doors into a spectacular drawing room. There was a terrace at the far side that overlooked the Grand Canal. And then doors that led down to what looked like a self-contained apartment at one side. Sarah's luggage and Nathan's bag were swept through to that side whilst Victoria's luggage was taken in the opposite direction.

She glanced through the door and saw a magnificent master bedroom with a massive four-poster bed. Its crisp white covers strewn with rose petals.

'We have left you and Signor Cavelli some champagne.' The manager indicated the magnum of champagne that sat in a silver ice bucket next to the bed, and there was a huge bouquet of flowers on the dressing table. 'With our best wishes, to you both.'

'Thank you…that's very kind.' Victoria could feel herself getting rather hot and uncomfortable as she noticed that some of Antonio's belongings were already in the room. By the looks of things he stayed here quite a lot. One of his suits was hanging over the trouser press. And there were some male toi-letries on a glass shelf. The hotel staff were obviously under the illusion that they were going to be sharing and using the room as a honeymoon suite.

She wanted to put them right at once, wanted to say, *You've made a mistake* and *Where am I to sleep?* But she didn't dare. Not when they had gone to all this trouble. It would probably be best to allow Antonio to sort out the misunderstanding later, she reassured herself. 'So has…my…husband arrived yet?'

It felt really strange referring to Antonio as her husband—she couldn't quite get used to it.

'No, signora, unfortunately he has been delayed, but he has left a message to say he will see you downstairs in the grand reception area of the foyer at eight o'clock.'

'Very well, thank you.'

The man bowed his head. 'If there is anything else you want, please do not hesitate to just lift the telephone.'

As the staff retreated, and Sarah busied herself bathing and changing Nathan into his pyjamas, Victoria hung her dress up on the outside of the wardrobe door and looked at it.

To a casual onlooker it would have seemed that every-thing was calmly under control, but inside Victoria was feeling anything but calm; she was feeling more and more apprehensive.

Her eyes flicked over the dress. In a moment of madness she had chosen to buy the halter-neck maxi dress. The material and the design were exquisite. It was a dress that made a stylish statement, a dress to be worn by a beautiful woman with a perfect body…

What had she been thinking?

It had seemed such a good idea yesterday…but today with the thought of Antonio waiting for her downstairs it scared her rigid.

But there was no time to change her mind now, she told herself fiercely, no plan-B dress to change into. She lifted her chin and told herself not to be foolish. So what if Antonio didn't like it—she had loved it when she tried it on, had been quite surprised by how good she had felt.

With more positive energy she sat down at the dressing table and opened her bag to unpack her toiletries and find her contact lenses.

She'd bought the lenses a long time ago so that she could wear sunglasses but had only worn them once. She hoped she would be able to put them in.

As eight o'clock approached, Victoria stepped back and looked in the mirror. She hardly recognised herself.

Antonio was in the lobby talking to the hotel manager. He'd had a busy day and because he'd been running late he'd had to shower and change into his dark tuxedo at his apartment in Verona. He'd only just made it here on time; they had to be in the ballroom at the Hotel Carnival in about twenty minutes so that he could give his welcoming speech. Luckily it was only a short stroll away but they needed to leave immediately.

'Did you give my wife the message about meeting me down here?' he asked the manager as he glanced at his watch.

'Yes, signor, and may I say again how happy we all are for you both? Signora Cavelli is a very beautiful woman.'

'Yes…thank you.' Distractedly Antonio looked at his watch again.

It was exactly eight; the clock in the main reception area was chiming the hour, its silvery notes resonating down the grand marble halls.

Antonio turned and looked towards the staircase that led to the lifts. There was a beautiful woman walking down. He watched her with extreme interest. She was absolutely breathtaking. Tall and elegant, she was wearing a shimmering halterneck dress that showed off her incredible figure to perfection. Her dark hair fell in a gleaming silken ripple of waves to one side of her lovely face. Her wide green eyes were framed with sweeping dark lashes, and she had a perfect mouth…a mouth that was made for kissing.

She smiled at him and he couldn't help but smile back, then he looked away. It was only as he looked away that he realized that there was something memorable about that smile…and the way she held herself. He looked back towards her with a feeling of incredulity. It was Victoria…. *It was his wife!*

In stunned amazement he watched the rest of her progress down the curving stairway, allowing himself to look at her with open curiosity now.

It took all of her courage to maintain her poise. When Antonio had first turned and looked at her, the boldness of his gaze had taken her breath. A man had never looked at her like that before, let alone a man who was so attractive. She could see the stunned recognition in his eyes now, and she could feel the shy burning feeling of pleasure inside of her intensifying a millionfold.

As she reached the last step, he walked across to meet her, his gaze moving with open unwavering approval down over the curves of her body.

'Victoria, you look amazing,' he murmured.

As her eyes locked with his she could see desire…and it scared her, but it also excited her.

'I wondered what lay beneath all those prim and proper outfits…' he murmured, and once more his attention wandered down over the delicious line of her neck and shoulders to linger on the firm uptilt of her full breasts. 'And…wow…'

Had she rendered the powerful and articulate Antonio Cavelli speechless? The knowledge gave her a swirling heady feeling of satisfaction and confidence, mixed with a deeply disturbing thrust of something else, some long-forgotten answering need that was invading her senses with increasing intensity.

With difficulty she tried to dismiss the feeling and smile with cool dignity. 'I'm glad you approve.'

Her answer and the way she looked at him just seemed to

feed the flame of interest inside of him all the more. He wanted her—wanted to unwrap her very, very slowly and kiss every last piece of her before he possessed her totally.

The sudden thought shocked him! That was out of the question, he reminded himself angrily. They had a business agreement and feelings like that were just going to complicate things far too much!

'We should go,' he said impatiently. 'The hotel is only a few minutes away. So I thought we'd walk if that's OK?'

'Yes, that's fine. I'd like some fresh air.'

He held out his arm for her and as they walked from the hotel together Antonio noticed the admiring glances thrown in their direction. In particular he noticed the way men looked at Victoria, their eyes hot with approval. She seemed totally oblivious of the fact and for some reason that made him want to hold her closer and more protectively to him....

He frowned at the thought. What on earth was wrong with him! He wasn't the possessive type—never had been, *never would be*—and certainly not over Victoria! When the time came and he had his shares in the company he would say goodbye to her....

Outside, the streets were dark, lit by the glitter of lanterns that sparkled down over the silky waters of the Rialto.

Antonio liked Venice by night, liked the sleepy pace after the hoards of day trippers had left; it was almost as if the city had slipped quietly back into a bygone era of less frenetic pace. And walking through the streets with Victoria at his side, he saw the place afresh through her eyes. She was so enthusiastic about everything that it was impossible not to get swept up in her excitement and enjoy the evening all the more.

Pigeons scattered as their footsteps echoed through one of the squares. Then they turned and walked over one of the small bridges. They could hear the distant sound of opera music coming from an open window above their heads.

'Puccini,' Victoria exclaimed with pleasure. 'That piece is

so lovely…and it just seems to fit here, as if it belongs with the bridges and the squares and cathedrals.'

He smiled at that and thought that the sparkle of enjoyment in her eyes was even lovelier.

Instinctively he put a hand around her waist to steady her as they walked over some cobbles.

'You'll have to be careful around here in such high heeled shoes.'

'Thanks!' She tried to sound nonchalant but his hand on her waist was having the strangest effect on her.

The delicate silk of her dress was so thin that it was almost as if he was touching her bare skin.

He pulled her a little closer. 'You know you blew me away when I watched you walk down that staircase tonight,' he told her softly.

'You thought I had no sense of style and that I'd look a complete frump tonight, I take it.' She tried to sound flippant.

'I don't know what I thought.' He stopped walking and looked down at her. 'I knew you could look good, and I've thought from the moment I met you that you could make more of yourself… Well, I told you what I thought…'

'Yes and I don't want to hear it again, thank you!' she said angrily.

He smiled at that. 'That's what I like about you, Victoria, that feisty manner. You have a lot of spirit hidden beneath that…rather delectable body…' His gaze flicked down over her and suddenly she could feel the atmosphere between them changing to the consistency of liquid heat.

She was forbidden fruit, Antonio reminded himself…but he couldn't help remembering how good it had felt to kiss her.

Had he imagined that?

His gaze lingered on the softness of her lips.

'We should go, otherwise we'll be late.' Her voice was husky and uncertain.

She was wondering about it, too—he just knew it.

'Victoria, about that kiss the other night—'

'I don't think we should talk about that.' Instantly she sounded embarrassed.

He smiled teasingly. 'I was just going to say it was surprisingly pleasurable.'

'Was it? I didn't notice.' She forced herself to try and sound glib but suddenly she ached for him to lean closer, to hold her, and to take possession of her lips. The intensity of that feeling made her freeze inside, because it was crazy and it would only lead to heartache—she knew the score.

'You didn't notice?' He sounded amused.

'No…not really.' Fiercely she tipped her chin up and met his gaze.

'Must have been my imagination then…or maybe we should try it again—see what happens?'

'We can't…' Her heart was pounding against her ribs now.

'There is no such thing as can't.' He stroked a stray strand of her hair back from her face and the gesture made the ache inside of her turn to a burning chasm.

Then he lowered his head and kissed her. For an instant she tried to pull away, but he held her firm, his mouth taking full possession of hers in a dominant way that made her senses spin. And she realized she didn't want to pull back; she realized she wanted this…wanted him.

The kiss was no gentle exploration of feeling; it was full-on intense passion—and the sensation was even more pleasurable than last time. Desire flooded through her so powerfully that it shook her to her core. She felt as if her body was wakening up, coming alive after a long winter in hibernation. She wanted to move even closer; she wanted so much more.

The sound of people approaching made them break apart. And she stared up at him as reality returned and consternation replaced passion.

'We shouldn't have done that,' she whispered.

The people they had heard were walking around the corner

now, their voices and their laughter sounding unnaturally loud in the stillness of the night. They passed by and Victoria was vaguely aware of the swish of long ball gowns and the smell of expensive perfume.

Then they were alone again.

What was Antonio thinking? she wondered as she looked up at him. His features were so inscrutable.

'Maybe you're right—we shouldn't have done that,' he agreed easily. 'However, don't try and tell me that you didn't enjoy it because I won't believe you.'

He was so damn arrogant! She forced herself to keep her head held high. 'I wasn't going to say that…. Actually, I was going to say that the ambience of our surroundings is obviously having an effect. But it's still a foolish mistake.'

He smiled suddenly, his dark eyes teasing. 'As foolish mistakes go—very enjoyable.'

There were more people coming along the path now. 'Come on. We'll talk about this later.' He reached out and took hold of her hand and they continued walking.

'I'd rather just forget it.' Even as she said the words she was aware that the touch of his hand was sending conflicting thoughts racing through her. Hastily she pulled away from him.

Antonio wasn't used to women doing that. But she was probably right. He knew that he was on dangerous territory with this. They had an agreement and he didn't want to complicate that. However, the more she tried to back away from him, the more he wanted to reel her in—why was that? He frowned. Was it simply the thrill of the chase…something he wasn't used to?

As they turned the corner Victoria saw the Grand Hotel Carnival; it was an impressive building on three levels with floodlit terraces that looked down over the canal.

Inside the doorway there was a vast stone-floored reception area filled with the buzz and laughter of hundreds of people.

Antonio's arrival was greeted with an excited commotion

and as they made their way through the crowds everyone seemed to want to claim his attention and speak to him.

Finally they got to the entrance of the ballroom. Ornate crystal chandeliers dazzled the senses. On a stage to one side, an orchestra was playing a Viennese waltz, whilst on the dance floor people were spinning around to the swell of the music.

They were directed towards a red-carpeted stairway that led to an upper gallery and a private table.

'This is a fantastic place,' Victoria remarked as Antonio pulled out a chair for her.

He leaned closer and she could smell the scent of his cologne. It reminded her of the heat of his kiss, and sent her emotions racing. But she needed to forget all about that, she told herself crossly.

He nodded. 'Yes, the building goes back to about the fifteenth century, I believe.'

Some waiters arrived with a magnum of champagne and placed two long-stemmed glasses down by the table.

They were going to pour the drink but Antonio dismissed them and reached to do it himself.

He raised his glass to hers. 'To a successful evening,' he said with a smile.

Some of the organizers came over to speak to him and he stood. 'I'm going to have to go and do my bit,' he told Victoria reluctantly. 'I won't be long.'

'OK.' She smiled and then leaned over the balcony to watch as he made his way downstairs and over towards the stage.

As he stood before the auditorium the music came to a crescendo and then stopped, and he was greeted with a tumultuous round of applause as everyone turned to look at him.

Victoria couldn't understand a word he said, but she felt a delicious curling sensation of excitement as she listened to the sexy timbre of his Italian tones. It was an excitement she didn't want to feel, and desperately she tried to shut it out, just as she tried to shut out the memory of that kiss. It shouldn't have happened. And if she allowed herself to get carried away with this situation she would just be storing up heartache. OK, Antonio thought she looked pretty tonight but that was just a whimsical passing moment on his part—he wasn't interested in the real her.

She watched as an attractive woman joined him onstage. She had long blonde hair and wore a dress that left little of her perfect body to the imagination.

Even a woman as beautiful as that would stand little chance of capturing Antonio's heart, she realized. He wasn't interested in commitment; he'd made that very clear right from the start. It was probably the main reason he had chosen to marry her—because he didn't want anyone who would get carried away with the role. So allowing reality to blur now would be a vast mistake and could only end in heartache. And she'd been there and got that particular T-shirt.

The auditorium was erupting into applause now as the woman kissed Antonio on both cheeks and they stepped down from the stage. Immediately Antonio made his way back to her, but it was a slow process as people kept stopping him to talk to him. Finally he reached the steps and returned to his chair. 'It is a very successful night, I think.'

She smiled and raised her glass. 'Well, it sounded good, but do I get a private translation?'

'Now that is a suggestion I like the sound of.'

The husky teasing tone made her blush and he laughed. 'We've exceeded last year's charity total by almost double. So it is a good night for the trust.'

'What charity is it for?'

'Children who are terminally ill. It's a cause that's close to my heart as I had a younger sister, Maria, who died of leukaemia when she was just six.'

'I didn't realize…I'm so sorry!' She looked at him in consternation.

'It happened over twenty-four years ago.' He smiled.

'They've made tremendous strides in treating the disease now.
I think she would have made a recovery if it had been in
today's world.'

'It must have been a terrible time.'

'Yes, it was, particularly for my mother.' For a moment he
looked serious, the handsome features lost in thought. 'Not
so much for my father, though. He seemed to find solace very
quickly in the arms of another woman.'

'Grief affects people in different ways,' she murmured softly.

He looked over at her and caught the gentle light of
sympathy in her eyes. 'Don't waste your compassion on him,
Victoria. Believe me, he's not worth it.'

'Actually, I was feeling sympathy for you,' she said quietly.

'Well, don't.' He frowned. 'It's a long time ago now.'

A long time ago but the scars still festered, she thought.
'Have you tried to talk to your father about what happened?'

He gave a short cold laugh. 'My father is not the type to talk
about his feelings.' He lifted his champagne and took a sip.
'And yes, grief affects people in different ways—some people
mourn and some people throw their families away.' He put the
glass down impatiently. 'So let's leave this subject, shall we?'

She nodded. Was the past the reason why he shunned commitment? she wondered. Had he watched his parent's
marriage fall apart and decided that there was no way he
wanted to go through that?

'Do you want to dance?' he asked abruptly.

She looked down towards the floor. The orchestra were
playing a slow number and couples were wrapped in each
other's arms. She would have loved to dance like that with
Antonio, but as she looked back and met the darkness of his
gaze she didn't dare.

'I think I'll sit this one out, thanks.'

He looked at her quizzically. 'Are you scared, Victoria?'

'No! Why would I be scared?'

His gaze drifted over her thoughtfully, noticing the clear

radiance of her skin and the defiant sparkle of her eyes. 'Sometimes I get the impression that someone did an almighty job of trying to crush your confidence.'

'Oh, really! What is this?' she countered, trying not to look in the slightest bit concerned. 'I've tried to analyse you, so now you are getting your own back?'

He laughed, and this time his laughter was warm and genuine. 'Maybe…' He held out his hand. 'Come on, come and dance. I dare you.'

She hesitated for a few seconds and then put her hand in his.

But it was a mistake. She knew as soon as they reached the dance floor and he gently pulled her closer that she should never have allowed him to provoke her into this.

Being held in his arms was too delicious. He made her feel cherished and protected…. He made her want him with a longing so deep that it hurt.

'You see…nothing terrible has happened—no lightning strikes, or thunder rolls,' he murmured, the teasing words soft against her ear.

Maybe not for him, she thought shakily. But it was taking all of her self-control not to turn her head and seek out his lips.

'Not a storm in sight,' she answered, closing her eyes. And for just a few precious moments she allowed herself to dream that Antonio really was her husband in every sense of the word. That it was safe to feel like this. Safe to lower her defences…*safe to love him*…

The thought made her pull away from him in shock. She didn't want to start imagining things like that! 'Antonio, I think I've had enough dancing,' she said hurriedly.

He frowned. But before he could say anything else she had turned away from him and left the floor.

He caught up with her just before she could head back to their table and put a hand on her shoulder to turn her towards him. 'What's the matter?'

'Nothing! I…I just can't dance in these heels.'

He didn't believe her. There was a note in her voice, a look in her eyes, that said much more than that, but there wasn't a chance of pursuing the question as some friends who had organized the evening came over to say hello.

Antonio introduced Victoria and found that he enjoyed the look of stunned amazement on people's faces when he told them she was his wife.

'How could you keep a secret like this from us?' He was chastised and congratulated in equal measure and Victoria was warmly welcomed. But it put an end to their evening alone, because after that everyone wanted to meet her and talk to her. And before he knew what was happening she was talking to one group and he was talking to another.

Out of the corner of his eye he noticed that although she checked her phone from time to time in case Sarah had been trying to reach her about Nathan, she seemed to be having a good time. Maybe she hadn't been upset earlier, because all her conversations now were lively and full of fun. Everyone liked her, he noticed. Especially some of his bachelor friends who were hanging on her every word with open admiration in their eyes.

Where was the shy young woman he had met just over a week ago? he wondered sardonically. She seemed to have morphed into a sophisticated, confident and beautiful young woman right before his very eyes.

As soon as he could he excused himself and sought her out. 'Having a good time?'

She smiled up at him. 'I'm really enjoying myself. Your friends are all very nice.'

'Yes, although I have to warn you there are a couple of my single friends over there that you can't trust.' He nodded towards the two men who had been asking her if she wanted to dance.

'Womanisers like you, are they?' She couldn't resist the teasing question.

'No, nothing like me,' he said with a smile. 'Because I'm a married man now, remember?'

'Ah, yes, and counting down the days to freedom.' She said the words as a joke, but they instantly jarred with her, and as their eyes met she wished that she hadn't said them. But they were probably true, she reminded herself firmly, forcing herself to face facts. 'So…how many days do you think that's going to be?'

The question irritated him. 'As many days and weeks as it takes.'

'OK…I'm not complaining. I…just wondered.' She looked up at him with those wide green eyes that were vulnerable and yet wary, and he felt a twist of some very strange emotion.

'Come on, I think it's time we called it a night. I don't know about you, but I've had enough.'

She nodded.

It was a relief to follow him out of the packed room into the coolness of the night. And when she looked at her watch she found with a surprise that it was after midnight.

They strolled back along the quiet streets without saying much, and this time Antonio didn't put an arm around her waist when they reached the bridge where he'd kissed her.

For a moment the memory of that kiss taunted her. How was it he was able to set her on fire so easily? Maybe she'd been right when she'd said that the mood and the ambience of the place had affected them. But then what was their excuse for the time before? Angrily she tried to clear the questions from her mind. It had just been a crazy moment and she was sure he was regretting it as much as her.

They reached the hotel and the night porter wished them a polite good-evening and went ahead of them to open the lift doors.

And then they were alone in the penthouse suite.

CHAPTER ELEVEN

'WOULD you like a nightcap?' Antonio moved towards the sideboard and picked up a decanter.

'No, thanks, I'm going to go and check on Nathan and then turn in for the night.' Victoria suddenly remembered that all her belongings were in with Antonio's in the master suite. And just the thought of that bed strewn with all those rose petals made her heart give an uneven little beat of consternation. 'Oh, I forgot to tell you!' She tried to keep her voice casually light. 'I think we might have a problem with the sleeping arrangements.'

'What kind of a problem?' He flicked an amused look over at her.

'The staff have put my things in with yours in the master suite. I would have moved them out,' she told him hurriedly, 'but there doesn't seem to be another spare bedroom up here.'

'I see.' He sounded unconcerned.

She stood uncertainly, wondering if he was going to say anything else, point her in the direction of where he wanted her to sleep, but he didn't. 'OK…well, I'll just go and check on Nathan.'

She'd hoped that when she returned he might have sorted the arrangements out but it didn't look as if he had done anything. Instead he was sipping a whisky and standing with his back to her, looking nonchalantly out towards the terrace.

'How's Nathan?' He turned as she walked back in.

'He's fine, fast asleep.'

'Good.'

She couldn't stop her eyes from flicking to the open doorway through to the master suite.

He intercepted the glance and she cringed. 'Have you seen the room? The staff really have got the wrong idea,' she told him huskily.

'Hmm.' He sipped his drink.

Was that all he was going to say? Anger started to build inside of her. 'You could ring down to reception and ask if they have another room, couldn't you?' she countered. 'There must be loads of spare rooms in a hotel this size.'

'I hope not,' he said quietly. 'It would be very bad for business if the hotel was that quiet!'

'Well, yes…I suppose it would,' she mumbled. 'So…what do you want to do?'

He looked at her playfully. 'Well, now, there is an interesting question…or is it an offer?'

'No!' Her cheeks flared with colour. 'Of course it isn't! You are too full of yourself by far, Antonio Cavelli.'

'Am I?' He just looked more amused than ever. And she tried to gather herself together.

'Yes, you damn well are! And…and let me tell you that I wouldn't want to sleep with you…if…if my life depended on it! Really I wouldn't.' She raised her chin defiantly.

'Really.' He put his drink down with a smile.

'Yes!' She glared at him. 'Now I'm going to bed…on my own…in the master bedroom.'

'Oh, I'm not so sure about that.' He reached out and stopped her before she could move past him and suddenly she was far too close to him.

'Don't, Antonio,' she whispered, her heart racing with agitation and sudden fear.

'Don't what?' He reached out and softly traced a finger over the curve of her chin.

'Don't play games with me.' The whispered plea tore at him.

Suddenly the confident person of tonight seemed to have vanished and in her place was the vulnerable young woman he had first met, who had looked at him with such fragile eyes.

He said something in Italian under his breath. 'I shouldn't tease you like this…should I?'

'No, you definitely shouldn't.' She tried to remain angry but the way he was looking at her was sending her senses in a different direction. 'We don't want to complicate things, Antonio. And if you and I ended up in bed together it would be a total disaster.'

'Absolutely,' he murmured, his eyes on her lips. 'It's not part of the deal at all.'

'No, it's not!' Her voice trembled. The way he was looking at her was shaking her up in the strangest way. 'And we are going to go our separate ways very soon.'

'That's the agreement…' His finger had moved to trace the curve of her lips and he only seemed to be half listening to her.

The caress sent an erotic shiver straight through her and desperately she tried to pull away from him and dismiss it, but her limbs wouldn't obey.

'Much better that we at least remain friends after our time together is finished,' she murmured. 'And sex is highly over-rated anyway.'

She had his full attention now.

'So how many lovers have you had, Victoria?'

'That's…none of your business!' Her skin was suddenly on fire.

He ran a finger over the smooth line of her shoulder and the feeling from that one light touch was so exquisite that it made her whole body tingle with pleasure. 'So you don't like sex at all?'

Her blood seemed to be too hot in her veins now! 'I said

it was overrated, nothing else. And I don't want to have this discussion, Antonio,' she murmured, desperate to just drop the subject.

'Maybe you just haven't gone to bed with the right man—have you ever thought about that?' he continued as if she hadn't spoken.

'And you are a very conceited man,' she retorted. 'Have *you* ever thought about that?'

He smiled, unconcerned by the charge, and continued to run his fingers lightly over her shoulder. 'But the thing is, you are presenting me with quite a challenge, Victoria Cavelli,' he murmured.

'Well, that's not my intention!' Her eyes snapped open.

'Nevertheless…I am very curious now.'

'Well, I don't want you to be.' Her eyes flared with fire.

'But I can't help it.' He smiled. 'You've set me thinking…' He bent and touched his lips to her shoulder, gently licking and tasting her skin in a way that made her eyes close on a sweep of fierce longing. 'Maybe you just need the right man to take things a little more slowly with you.'

'I don't want to take things slowly or an way at all…' Her breathing felt tight.

'What about the way you kissed me earlier?'

'That kiss was just a moment of madness. I thought we agreed that it was best forgotten!'

'Did we say that?'

'Yes, we did. We definitely agreed we wouldn't discuss it again.'

'Then if we can't discuss it, I will just have to experience it again…because I keep wondering if I am imagining your fiery passionate responses…and I'm just going to have to find out for myself what the truth is.'

'You mustn't, Antonio!' Her eyes widened. 'I mean it—'

The rest of her sentence was lost as he leaned down and took possession of her lips. The feeling was as sensational as it had been earlier, and desperately she tried to fight the emotions that flooded through her, but his mouth was hard and hungry and it demanded an urgent response.

And before she knew what she was doing she was winding her arms up and around his neck and kissing him back.

He pulled away and her eyes were shadowed as she looked up at him. The kiss had fragmented her already incoherent thoughts. 'I just don't think this is a good idea—'

'Maybe we are both thinking far too much.' Suddenly he swept her off her feet and up into his arms. 'Maybe we just need to explore the subject in much more detail.'

'Antonio, put me down this minute!'

He paid her no attention. And shocked, she was forced to hang onto him as he strode towards the bedroom.

'Put me down,' she asked again, but this time her tone had lost its vehement intent. Disturbingly she found she liked being held in his arms like this, that the feeling was sending a thrust of desire through her that was so strong it almost took her breath away.

Desperately she tried to hang onto the last semblance of sanity. 'This isn't a good idea.'

'Well, I think it is.' He closed the bedroom door behind him with his foot.

'Now…where were we,' he murmured as he put her down. 'I think it was somewhere around about here…' He bent and kissed her shoulder and then moved upwards. 'Wasn't it?'

She shuddered with pleasure and he smiled.

'Yes, we were definitely around about here….' He found the sensitive area of her neck and nuzzled in against her, biting her softly, peppering her with light kisses.

She'd never experienced anything as pleasurable before in her life and she was helpless to protest because the more he touched her, the more he kissed her, the more she wanted him. He pulled her a little closer and then unfastened the top of her dress with bold confident fingers.

'I've imagined doing this all evening,' he murmured as he watched the silky garment fall to the floor.

She was wearing lacy black underwear that hugged her curves provocatively.

'You really are beautiful....' His husky words made her close her eyes. She wanted to savour the moment; she wanted to believe that he really thought that about her, and that they weren't just the words of seduction. 'I don't know why you've hidden yourself away beneath all those shapeless clothes...' He reached out and trailed one hand down over the smooth line of her neck, and then lower to where the delicate lace held her curves. 'When you have such a fabulous body.'

Her eyes flew open as he teasingly stroked his fingers over the top of her bra. The sensual twist of need increased inside her.

Then his hand moved lower, curving around her breasts, moulding them with firm possessive strokes that nearly drove her out of her mind with need. He leaned closer and kissed her neck again, and suddenly even the flimsy scrap of lace across her breasts was too much of a barrier. She wanted him to pull it away; she wanted to feel his hands against her naked skin. But he didn't; he just stroked her, and murmured soft words against her ear as his hand moved lower over the narrow curve of her waist to the top of her lace pants.

'You have the figure of a voluptuous woman, and I want you to promise me that you will never hide yourself away again.'

'I haven't hidden myself away...' She tried to deny the accusation as a thrust of even deeper desire swept through her as his fingers moved lower over her pants.

'Yes, you have...and I want to know what moronic man made you do that!'

She laughed breathlessly at the growled words.

'You should be proud of your body....' His hands cupped around her hips and then slid below the string of her pants and stroked over her stomach, and then down towards the sensitive core of her.

'Now tell me that you want me and let's be done with pretence, hmm?' He said the words with commanding, arrogant confidence and she fought against answering him, but his hand was caressing her so provocatively that the fierceness of desire was pulsating through her.

'I want you!' The words broke in a gasp from her lips.

He covered her mouth with his, hungrily kissing her as his fingers probed with firmer, deeper strokes.

For a long moment she could think of nothing except the demanding needs of her body. It had never been like this with Lee.... The thought encroached and he pulled back slightly.

'What's the matter?' He saw the shadows in her eyes.

'I'm just a little scared,' she admitted, her barriers crumbling her dignity and her pride deserting her. 'I'm not experienced, Antonio. I know it sounds stupid—I have a child, but...' Her voice trailed away as she remembered the past. 'I went out with a man once, for several months, but we didn't sleep together straight away—it just never felt the right time. And then when I did...it was awful, Antonio.' Her voice broke. 'He got angry because I was a virgin, said that he liked his women more experienced, and then he just took me without any thought and then it was all over...' She saw the way his eyes darkened angrily.

'I know you are probably used to women who know how to please you but—'

He placed a finger over her lips. 'You do please me, with every kiss, with every look and word.' He stroked a hand through her hair, hating to think about what she had gone through that night and later, alone and pregnant. No wonder she was so scared. He muttered something angrily in Italian. Then he kissed her again and this time his lips were gentle and probing. And for a long while he just held her close.

Then he reached behind her and unfastened her bra. 'I will teach you in the ways of lovemaking, Victoria...'

Usually Antonio's English was perfect but now as passion

overtook him he spoke half in Italian, half in English…his words punctuated with caresses that made her ache with pleasure.

He lifted her and put her down on the bed and she watched as he took off his clothes.

He had a fabulous body, lean and powerfully muscular.

She looked away as he caught her watching him and he laughed. 'You mustn't be shy with me, Victoria. It's not allowed.' He joined her on the bed. 'I want you to tell me exactly what you like, or if you don't like something, and we'll find the way to a perfect union…hmm?' As he spoke his eyes were on her breasts, admiring their pert ripe form. He reached out and stroked them, finding the hardened peaks of her nipples. Then he bent his head and allowed his mouth to replace his fingers.

She gasped with enjoyment as the warmth of his mouth seemed to pervade the whole of her body, and she reached out and raked her fingers over his shoulders, bending her head and burying her face in the thickness of his hair, breathing in the fresh scent of his shampoo….

Then he was bringing her back down on the bed, straddling her, his hands moving down over her possessively as his lips moved lower down over her stomach, his hands stroking lower.

He pulled her pants down impatiently and she wiggled out of them.

Then his hand moved between her thighs, parting her legs as his mouth moved down, kissing her playfully over her lower abdomen, then lower…lower…

The ache inside of her became a roaring torrent of need.

'I want you, Antonio… I need you now…' Was that husky pleading voice hers?

He sat back and looked at her. Her hair was loose around her shoulders; her face was flushed, her lips swollen from his kisses.

He stroked one hand over her breast and she arched her back like a cat, inviting him to stroke her further.

He thought he had never seen a woman more lovely, more alive and warm and passionate. He stroked her some more.

'Tell me again, how much you want me,' he invited playfully.

How could she have lost control like this? She tried to caution herself. She shouldn't be giving herself like this to him when he didn't love her. Where was her pride? *She'd promised herself she wasn't going to do this!*

But she was weak.… She wanted him…she loved him.

The words shook her. But they were no real shock. Deep down she'd always known how she felt, known it as soon as she first saw him. It was what had terrified her so much…

'I need you, Antonio…' she whispered. 'I need you, now!'

He pulled her further down in the bed, positioning her exactly as he wanted her, stroking her, kissing her, a feeling of triumphant elation hitting him as he realized she was his, to do as he wanted with.

When she woke up, Antonio was still asleep beside her. And she lay watching him as dawn crept into the room. Their night together had been the most wonderful night she had ever experienced and she didn't regret it. Would never regret it—no matter what happened now, she told herself vehemently. Because he had shown her how truly amazing lovemaking could be. He'd been passionate and caring, had taken control when it most mattered, and had made sure he'd protected her from pregnancy by wearing something. The whole experience had been…perfect.

Well, it would have been perfect if he had uttered one little word of love. But she couldn't expect that; she knew the score, knew that last night was about passion, not love and, when the time came, Antonio would let her go. She wasn't totally naive!

But she wasn't going to think about that now, she told herself hurriedly. She was just going to enjoy what time they had together.

For a few moments she allowed her gaze to roam over him. He was so handsome, she thought. His features were aristocratic, yet rugged. She noticed the dark stubble on his jaw line, the fine grain of his skin, the thick dark lashes, the sensual curve of his lips...lips that had given her so much pleasure.

Maybe it was best not to think about that now, she told herself with a smile, because if she did she'd want him all over again, and in a few moments she'd have to get up and see to Nathan.

Reluctantly she rolled over and reached for her dressing gown.

'Where are you going?' he murmured sleepily.

'Nathan will be waking up around now and he'll want his breakfast.' She looked back at him shyly and felt herself blushing as his gaze moved boldly over her naked body.

'OK...I guess that I'll allow you to go in that case.' He smiled sleepily as he watched her through hooded eyes. 'But be warned, I'll want you back again a little later—my appetite will take a lot more satisfying.'

He laughed as she blushed even more. Then as she made to put her dressing gown on he put an arm around her waist and pulled her back in against him. 'You forgot something...'

'Have I?' She looked around at him, her heart pounding as if she had been running in several long races. 'What have I forgotten?'

'This.' He leaned closer and kissed her, a long lingering seductive kiss that melted her completely. 'My morning kiss,' he told her, releasing her. 'I'd like another around midmorning, and another couple this afternoon.'

'That could be arranged,' she said, smiling.

'Good, now go and see to Nathan.' He leaned back against the pillows. 'Oh, and look on the menu outside and phone downstairs and order breakfast.'

'What would you like?'

'Anything, I'm ravenous!'

As she met the gleam in his dark eyes she laughed breathlessly. She was quite hungry herself.

When she left the room, Antonio lay where he was for a moment, then threw the covers back and went for a shower.

No point analysing what had happened, he told himself briskly. They'd had sex and it had been very enjoyable.

A little later, showered and changed, Antonio went through into the apartment.

It was a bright sunny morning and Victoria was sitting outside on the terrace. She was feeding Nathan, who was sitting beside her in a high chair.

They made an interesting picture and for a moment he allowed himself to watch her unobserved. She looked radiantly lovely, her dark hair spilling down over the blue of her gown, her eyes focused on her son as she held the spoon out to him.

Nathan was kicking his feet impatiently and trying to take the spoon away from her.

'No, Nathan, eat your porridge for Mummy like a good boy.'

The child shook his head and kept his mouth tightly closed and she laughed. 'Come on, honey... Look, it's like the helicopter we were in yesterday. Around and around it goes and...open wide...' She swooped around with the spoon and tried to get him to take it but he steadfastly refused.

'Looks like you are fighting a losing battle,' Antonio observed, and she turned around in surprise.

'I didn't realize you were there.'

'I was enjoying the helicopter show. But I think you'll have to come up with a different plan.' He sat down at the table and reached for the coffee pot.

She glanced over at him distractedly. He looked very stylish in a dark suit and a white shirt that was open at the neck. Had this handsome Italian really made love to her, over and over again as he'd told her how beautiful she was? The memories made her go weak inside. It didn't feel real—it felt like some kind of dream.

'Come on, Nathan, eat some breakfast for Mummy...' She tried to concentrate.

'Here, let me.' Antonio leaned across and took the spoon. 'Nathan, eat some breakfast like a good boy…and later we will take you to the funfair.'

Her son was looking at him with wide eyes.

'You can drive a train or a little car all by yourself…if you're good.'

'That's bribery!' Victoria said with a shake of her head.

'Maybe, but it works.' He laughed as the child opened his mouth and took the food. 'Good boy.' He smiled over at Victoria. 'Some people have just got what it takes.'

'Have I told you that you're very conceited,' she asked playfully.

'Yes, a few times. You also told me last night that you knew why I was very conceited.' His eyes were warm and teasing and she blushed.

'Why don't you run along and get dressed and I'll take over here,' he said gently.

'Are you sure?' She frowned. 'Sarah has gone out. She wanted to do some shopping.'

'Yes, I've given her the day off. So run along. The sooner you get ready, the sooner we can go out.'

'Where are we going?'

He shook his head. 'I just told you—we're going to the funfair.'

'Oh! I thought that you were just…pretending.'

He raised one eyebrow. 'I rarely say things I don't mean, so off you go.'

She nodded and slowly got up from the table. 'So…don't you have to go to work today?'

He shook his head. 'No, it's my day off.'

'Oh.'

'If you say *oh* just one more time, I'm going to throw some of this porridge at you.'

'Please don't. That's Nathan's job.' With a grin she stood and kissed her son on the forehead. 'Be a good boy…I won't be long.'

She flicked a glance back before she went into the bedroom. It felt unreal watching Antonio feeding Nathan. He was a high-flying ruthless businessman, yet right now he seemed quite engrossed in the task of cajoling Nathan into eating his breakfast!

An onlooker might have thought that he was Nathan's father, she reflected. Immediately as the thought entered her head she dismissed it. He wasn't Nathan's father—and thoughts like that were far too dangerously provocative.

Antonio was a free spirit, and she had to remember that.

CHAPTER TWELVE

VICTORIA was in the garden with Nathan. The two of them had enjoyed lunch under the dappled shade of a lemon tree. And now Nathan was splashing in the little blow-up paddling pool that Antonio had bought for him.

He was having a great time, kicking away at the water, sending it whooshing out onto the grass and soaking himself in the process. He laughed up at Victoria.

'Yes, you are having great fun,' she said with a smile. 'You like that pool, don't you? Antonio knew what he was doing when he bought that for you.'

Nathan looked around as if Antonio was going to suddenly materialize. 'No, he's still at work, honey,' she murmured.

But he would be home soon, she told herself silently, and a little burst of joy erupted somewhere deep inside of her. She looked at her watch. It was almost two—he shouldn't be too long now.

Things had settled into a delightful routine over these past few weeks since their trip to Venice.

They'd been able to spend quite a lot of time together because Antonio wasn't so busy at work. He'd caught up on a lot of the backlog from when he was away and things at the office had quietened down so he was getting home earlier and earlier every day.

Sometimes he arrived when Nathan was having his afternoon nap and they would take advantage of the fact and have a siesta themselves. Just thinking about those languid afternoons making love in the cool of his bedroom made her turn to jelly inside.

Sometimes he would take them out. Yesterday they'd gone to Malcesine, a magical little village on the banks of Lake Garda. They'd explored the medieval castle and then Antonio had insisted on buying Nathan a gigantic ice cream whilst they'd sat at a café in the square. It had been fun sitting watching the world go by, just the three of them, in contented silence on a sleepy hot afternoon.

Victoria didn't think she had ever felt so happy.

And Nathan had loved every minute of their outings. But then he adored Antonio, seemed to almost hero-worship him.

She knew Antonio was just being kind and that he had no real feelings for her son and yet he was so gentle and patient that it made her love him all the more.

She heard the click of a gate as someone walked around from the front of the house and she looked over, hoping it would be Antonio.

But it wasn't. Instead an elderly man in a lightweight suit stood just under the trees. 'I was looking for Antonio,' he murmured in heavily accented English.

With a shock she realized that it was Antonio's father, and memories of that terrible night when she'd gone to his house came flooding back.

Hurriedly she got to her feet. 'He's not home yet.'

Luc Cavelli noticed how different she looked. There was still a look of wariness in her expression, but her general appearance was relaxed, her summer clothes feminine and fitted. Her hair was loose and she was wearing a trendy pair of designer glasses that suited her immensely. No wonder everyone who had seen her out and about with his son had told him she was beautiful.

He transferred his attention over towards Nathan as he continued to splash in the pool with unreserved enthusiasm. 'Your son seems to be enjoying himself,' he said with a smile.

'Yes.'

There was a moment's awkward silence between them. Victoria didn't know what to say to him.

'Well, I'm sorry I disturbed you.' He nodded politely and turned to go. 'Tell Antonio that I called, will you?'

'He shouldn't be long,' Victoria found herself saying impulsively. 'Do you want to sit and wait for him?'

Slowly the man turned back and looked at her.

At first she thought he wasn't going to accept, but then he inclined his head. 'That would be good. It's hot today, and I can't take the heat as much as I used to.' As he walked over and sat down at the table Victoria realized that he did look tired.

'Would you like a cold drink, Signor Cavelli? I have some freshly squeezed orange juice in the fridge. It's quite nice mixed with sparkling water.' She shrugged. 'Well, it's what I like to drink in the heat of the day.'

What was she prattling on about? she wondered nervously. This man probably hated her and wouldn't be in the slightest bit interested in what she liked to drink!

But to her surprise he smiled. 'That's very kind.'

'OK. Would you mind keeping an eye on Nathan for me?'

'No, I don't mind at all.' The man looked over towards the little boy, watching his youthful energy with interest. He'd also heard reports about the child—and about how much he looked like Antonio. There was a resemblance now he looked closer.

When Victoria returned a few moments later with the tray of drinks and some biscuits she found that Nathan had got out of the water and was showing Antonio's father his collection of inflatable toys. Everything was being dragged over, a big rubber ring, a giant red ball, a yellow duck.

'Oh, no, Nathan! They are all wet!' Hurriedly she put the

tray down on the table but it was too late. The dripping red ball was being firmly pushed onto the man's knee.

'It's OK, really!' Luc laughed as she rushed to take it away. 'A little water will soon dry in this heat.'

'Come and have a biscuit, Nathan, and leave Signor Cavelli in peace.'

'Call me Luc, please.' The man accepted the drink she poured out for him and then watched as the child settled onto her knee. 'I think you are the one who will be soaking wet,' he said.

She smiled as she looked down at her white skirt and short-sleeved blouse. 'I was splashed to high heaven anyway.'

Luc watched as Nathan happily munched on his biscuit. He noticed how dark his eyes were, how golden his skin. 'He's a fine child,' he said after a moment.

'Yes, I think so, but then I am biased.'

'He does look a little bit like Antonio,' he reflected suddenly, and then turned to look directly at her. 'Is he my son's child?'

'No.' Victoria shook her head, her cheeks suddenly flaring with colour. 'No, he's not.'

'Sorry, I shouldn't have asked.' The man muttered something in Italian under his breath. 'It was stupid of me! Antonio did tell me categorically that he wasn't his, when he brought you both to my house.' Luc shrugged. 'It's just that there is a resemblance.'

'Just the same dark hair and eyes, that's all.' Victoria picked up the plate of biscuits and offered him one. But he shook his head.

She wanted to change the subject—talk about anything else—but she couldn't think what to say. He was looking at her with such intensity.

'I have to apologise to you for my rudeness that night,' he said suddenly.

'I think that's probably best forgotten.' She flicked him a nervous look. She certainly didn't want to think about it. In fact, she wanted to close that whole chapter of her life and just start her memories here with Antonio at the ball in Venice.

'Well, that's more than I deserve.' He smiled at her. 'I was just so angry. I'd promised Antonio that I would hand over my shares in the business if he got married and produced a child. I meant that I wanted him to have his own child to ensure the future of the Cavelli bloodline. But I didn't word it like that in my correspondence.'

The words fell in the heat of the day like tiny shards of a bomb fragment.

'So Antonio produced us,' she said numbly as the last pieces of the charade fell into place. She supposed she'd always known deep down that it was something like that.

She remembered his words to her on the day he'd told her he wanted her for his wife.

I'm in need of a ready-made family for a short-term period without any strings or complications.

She swept an unsteady hand through her hair, trying to shut the memory out. She didn't want to remember what he'd said. Had been determinedly trying to close the facts out of her mind for weeks.

The man's tired gaze moved back to Nathan, who was sliding off her knee now to go back and pick up his toys.

'I shouldn't have taken my annoyance out on you,' Luc said softly. 'It was just when Antonio told me that night that he would never have his own child and that I would never pressurise him to making that kind of commitment, I was…livid.'

'I understand.' Victoria's voice was husky. She didn't want to understand; she wanted to close her ears and block out the truth. But she knew that was just stupid…just as it had been stupid of her to try and block out the truth about her marriage over these past few weeks. She'd lulled herself into a false sense of security! And now with every word that Luc Cavelli was uttering she realized how crazy that had been.

'Stupidly, when people reported seeing you out with my son—seeing…Nathan…' His gaze moved to the child. 'I had a wild hope that Antonio had been lying to me…but it was just wishful thinking.'

'He wouldn't have lied about something as important as that,' Victoria told him with raw pain in her eyes.

He nodded. 'Ah, well…such is life.' Once more the man looked over at Nathan. 'I have a lot of high-powered lawyers who are annoyed with me that I didn't consult them in the first instance over this issue, but to be honest I didn't have the— what is it you English say?—the *stomach* for it.'

'Lawyers can sometimes make things worse anyway,' Victoria murmured. 'I think you and Antonio would be better to talk honestly to each other.'

'Wise words. But unfortunately we have been too far apart for too long, and it's my fault, I admit.' Luc shook his head. 'But when I told Antonio that I wanted him to settle down and have a family I meant it sincerely. I'm getting old…and… well, Antonio doesn't know this but my health isn't good. Things like that make you re-evaluate your life and the things that are important. I've been taking a long hard look at myself and I honestly haven't liked what I've seen.'

'You should tell Antonio this,' Victoria advised.

'It's too late for that. I shouldn't have tried to force his hand the way I did. I've always been the same—I've done things to suit myself without thought. I can be too single-minded, too determined.'

'Sounds like the two of you are a lot alike,' she murmured, and he gave a grunt of laughter.

'Don't tell him that! My son isn't frightened of anything in life—apart from ever being like me.' He shook his head. 'And I can't say I blame him.'

Silence fell. 'You really should still try and talk to him,' she said after a moment as she remembered the sadness that had befallen their lives. 'People make mistakes.'

The man sighed. 'Anyway, I've come to tell him that I've transferred the shares over into his name. I did it this morning.'

Victoria couldn't find her voice to answer him. If Antonio had his shares, that meant he no longer needed her here. He'd been completely honest about that. What was it he'd said? *'As soon as my business transaction is completed we can have the marriage dissolved and go our separate ways—no need to see each other ever again.'*

Luc frowned suddenly. 'Are you OK? You look a little pale.'

She nodded and desperately tried to pull herself together. She'd known this moment would come. It was crazy to be upset.

Luc seemed about to say something else, but the sound of the gate opening behind them made them both look around.

It was Antonio and just the sight of him made her heart race with a need so deep that she hated herself for it.

She saw the look of surprise on his face when he noticed his father at the table—surprise and annoyance. But before he could say anything Nathan had scrambled out of the pool to run towards him with an excited whoop of delight.

With complete disregard for the fact that he would get his suit wet, Antonio scooped him up.

Watching them, Victoria felt as if someone had stabbed a dagger through her.

She shouldn't have allowed Nathan to get so attached to Antonio…*shouldn't have allowed herself to get so attached.*

'So what is going on here?' Antonio asked curtly, looking over towards his father.

'Your father has come to offer his apologies for…the other night and to talk to you.' Victoria got stiffly up from the table and with a smile in Luc Cavelli's direction she went to take her son from Antonio.

Nathan wasn't happy about being transferred, but Victoria ignored his cries. 'I'll leave you two to talk,' she told Antonio.

Nathan wailed all the way from the garden up to his nursery. 'Be a good boy for Mummy,' she told him softly.

She felt like crying too but she tried to focus on her child and on what was important.

It was time to go home. She had to be practical now.

The new restaurant was finished. The opening night was set for next week.

'Nathan, please stop crying,' she told him as she stripped him out of his wet togs.

She glanced out of the window down towards the garden. Antonio hadn't sat down at the table. His body language was confrontational.

She hoped that he would at least listen to his father. They needed to draw a line under the past before it was too late.

Victoria bathed and changed Nathan. He was getting tired now, ready for his afternoon nap. She put him down and he fell asleep without a murmur. Then she went through to Antonio's room and switched on the computer.

She didn't even realize what she was doing until she found herself looking at flights to Australia. There was one that left at eight-thirty tonight, but she would have to fly via Rome.

Staring at the itinerary she found her eyes blurring with tears. She didn't want to go! She rubbed at her eyes, trying desperately to get her thoughts under control. Maybe she should wait and talk to Antonio, sound him out as to what he was thinking.

Trouble was she had her pride. What could she say to him? *How do you feel about me?* She cringed. He'd probably say he enjoyed the sex but the status quo hadn't changed. That he didn't do commitment.

But after the time they'd shared these past few weeks, didn't she at least deserve to find out if that definitely was still the case?

The bedroom door opened suddenly and Antonio strolled in.

Hurriedly she pressed the sleep button on the computer so that the screen shut down, and then she stood. 'Has your father gone home now?'

'Yes. I'm glad to say.'

She watched as he put his jacket down on the bed and unfastened his tie. She could almost see the muscles rippling under his white shirt as his powerful body flexed.

No man had a right to be that good-looking, she told herself fiercely. She wished she didn't feel this pull of attraction for him, wished that her body would stop betraying her. She needed to be sensible.

'So how did it go?' she asked quietly.

He flicked her a quizzical look. 'Much the same way as it usually goes with him. He talked in riddles.'

'He was making perfect sense when he spoke to me. And I don't think he's very well.'

'Why, what's the matter with him?' Antonio looked over at her sharply, surprise in his dark eyes.

'I don't know, he didn't say.'

Antonio shook his head. 'He plays games, Victoria. He always has—don't be fooled.'

'So when he told me about the deal he drew up to give you his last remaining shares in the company if you married and had a child, he was lying?'

Antonio had been in the process of unbuttoning his shirt but he stopped now and looked over at her. 'He told you that?'

She nodded.

'He'd no right to do that!' He sounded blazingly angry suddenly.

'Why? Because it's not true?'

'It is true—'

'Oh, so it's because you consider this none of my business, I suppose?' she cut across him angrily and angled her chin up as she remembered him telling her that once.

'No. He shouldn't have told you because it wasn't his place to tell you!' His eyes narrowed on her. 'As I said, he plays games, tries to cause trouble, tries to force people to his way of thinking.'

She shrugged. 'Well, whatever he was doing, you've got your precious shares now, so I suppose that's all that matters.'

Was that all that mattered? Antonio stared at her, trying to get a handle on his thoughts. When he'd first started out with this he had certainly believed that. But he suddenly felt as if he was in uncharted territory now, and he really didn't like the feeling.

'So I've just been looking at flights to Australia on the Internet,' she continued.

'You haven't wasted much time!'

'Well, what did you expect me to do?' She forced herself to shrug. 'I mean, now that you have what you wanted, our business deal is at an end…isn't it?'

She waited for his reply, her heart thudding painfully hard against her chest.

Antonio thought about the question for a few moments. 'I guess it is,' he said slowly.

The answer hurt. But somehow she kept her head held high, kept her dignity. But it was a struggle.

'I've found a flight that leaves at eight-thirty tonight.' She swallowed hard, wanting him to tell her not to go, wanting this to be all right and for him to realize that really he couldn't live without her.

'Tonight?' He looked shocked and she felt a stab of hope.

'Yes, it's the earliest one I could find. It goes via Rome.'

'I don't think that's a good idea,' he said firmly. 'And anyway, you don't have to rush off so quickly.'

'Don't I?' She raised her eyes to his. 'Is there any reason why not?'

It was the nearest she could manage to asking him how she felt about her, without actually saying the words.

The question seemed to burn between them.

For a few precious heartbeats she hoped he was going to come closer, that he wanted to take her into his arms.

His dark eyes seemed to pierce through her.

'Things are okay the way they are.' He shrugged. 'I think we could let the situation continue for a while.'

Was that it? she wondered angrily. Was that the best he could do? Well, she thought she deserved more than that. 'I don't think that's a good idea, Antonio.' Her voice trembled. 'It's the opening night for my new restaurant next week and I would like to be there for it.' She started to turn away from him but he caught her wrist suddenly and pulled her back.

'The staff can see to that. You don't need to be there.'

The touch of his hand made her senses ache. She wanted to fold into his arms. She wanted to just say, *Yes, yes, OK, I'll stay here with you.* Wanted to take any scrap of affection that he could spare for her.

'We've been having a good time, haven't we? Why end it so abruptly?' he asked her huskily.

Their eyes locked.

It would be so easy to just agree. She wanted to so much… but then she remembered Nathan, remembered the joy in his eyes whenever he saw Antonio, remembered the way he looked for him and ran into his arms. The longer she stayed here the more attached her son would get to him. It wouldn't be fair. She had to put Nathan first. At least now he was still so young that he would forget Antonio relatively quickly—the older he got, the harder it would be.

'Yes, we've had a good time.' Her eyes were filled with the intensity of her emotions. 'But a good time isn't enough for me, Antonio. I have a child—I need to think sensibly about where this is going…for both of our sakes.'

He frowned and allowed his hand to drop from her wrist. 'You know I can't make you promises, Victoria….'

'I know.' She looked away from him and swallowed on the tears that wanted to rise in her throat. 'And I have to go home, Antonio.'

CHAPTER THIRTEEN

As VICTORIA made her way across the crowded restaurant, people stopped her to congratulate her on the evening. The food was fabulous, they said, and the ambience perfect.

'We've done it,' her head chef, Berni, gushed in delight as she walked through to the kitchen. 'We've pulled it off. The opening night is a complete success and we are now on the map as the place to dine in Sydney.'

'Well…let's not get too carried away, Berni,' she said cautiously. 'It's just the first night.'

'No, you don't understand.' He caught her by the hand and led her towards the doorway. 'Do you see that man sitting over by the window—that's Paul Scott, one of *the* most revered food critics in the business. And he just called me over to tell me he loved everything about his dining experience here tonight and for us to read his review in the *Daily Journal* tomorrow.'

'Really!' Victoria turned wide eyes on her chef and he laughed.

'Yes, really. We are absolutely made!'

She smiled, and tried to get some real enthusiasm into her voice. She should be thrilled. What the hell was the matter with her? she wondered angrily. 'Well, listen, I'm just going to go and take a break and check with the babysitter that all is fine with Nathan. I won't be a minute.'

'It's OK, you don't need to rush. The crowd is thinning out now. It's all under control here.'

'Thanks, Berni.' She headed out of the side door and up the steps to the terrace of her apartment.

It was a relief to be outside in the warmth of the evening air. And for a moment she stood looking down at her restaurant. She could see the candlelight flickering on the tables, could hear the faint strains of music from the quartet she'd hired for the evening. They were playing Puccini, and she had a sudden memory of that night in Venice when Antonio had kissed her.

She should have told them not to play that! She'd been trying so hard not to think about Antonio. She didn't need or want him in her life, she told herself staunchly.

The distant lights of Sydney Harbour glittered and blurred against the velvet darkness of the sky and she blinked furiously. She wouldn't cry; he wasn't even worth that—and besides, she'd lose her contact lenses.

A warm breeze rustled through the bougainvillea and the jasmine that covered the terrace where she and Nathan sat to have their breakfast.

She took a deep breath of the scented air and gathered herself back under control.

She should be happy her new restaurant was a success; she was a woman of independent means. OK, Antonio had bank-rolled her but it was only what he owed her after ousting her from her last property. And she'd pay back the money that he'd advanced to get her going. Would pay it back with interest because she really didn't want to be beholden to him.

She was going to be able to run her own life efficiently from now on, she reminded herself firmly. She and Nathan didn't need Antonio Cavelli.

From now on there would be no regrets. She couldn't allow herself to remember the wonderful times in his arms. Or the way he'd swung Nathan into the air and laughed with them.

It hurt too much. Instead she needed to remember that warm Italian evening when he had calmly let her go.

'You know I can't make you promises, Victoria....'

The words echoed through her mind angrily now. He'd sent Sarah up to help her pack and then he had calmly gone out.

Sarah had been distraught. 'Why are you going, signora?' she had asked her. 'You will be coming back?'

'I don't think so, Sarah... This marriage was never meant to be. You know that.'

'No! You and Antonio are perfect together and if he lets you go it's because he's too stubborn and afraid to admit it.'

'Antonio isn't afraid of anything. He just doesn't want me. If he did he would be here with me now. He wouldn't have sent you.'

The woman hadn't been able to say anything to that. Because deep down she must have known Victoria was right. Sarah had cried when the limousine had arrived to collect her. Had hugged Nathan fiercely.

Just thinking about it now made Victoria's eyes fill with tears again.

So no, she wasn't going to remember Antonio with sentimental thoughts. She was going to stay angry. He was cold and emotionless. He thought by throwing money at a problem it made everything all right.

When she'd arrived at the airport she'd found he'd upgraded her to first class. She supposed he thought that made everything better!

Well, it didn't.

He'd also sent a magnificent bouquet of flowers for her tonight. With a card that read, *Thinking of you tonight. Good luck. Antonio.*

She was filled with a furious stabbing pain now as she thought about it. How dare he send her flowers and wish her well so...flippantly!

He was patronizing, arrogant—hateful!

She'd thrown the bouquet out in a fit of temper. He could keep his damn flowers!

Hurriedly she turned and went up and into her apartment. Margaret, her babysitter, was sitting watching TV in the open-plan lounge.

'Is everything OK?' She jumped up as Victoria came in.

'Yes, you relax. I'm just having a quick break and I thought I'd check on Nathan.'

'He's fast asleep.'

'I'll just pop my head around the door anyway.'

The only time she felt happy these days was with her son. She leaned against the cot and looked down at the sleeping child, gathering her strength.

Even he had missed Antonio. She'd taken him to the park yesterday and they'd eaten ice cream and then Nathan had turned and said Antonio's name. He couldn't quite pronounce it and it had come out as Anio.

'Anio is not here, darling,' she'd told him softly. 'He's at his house in Italy.'

Nathan had looked upset—and that had torn her apart even more.

But it just went to show that she'd done the right thing in coming back here. The longer she'd stayed with Antonio, the harder this would have been.

She pressed a kiss on his forehead and told herself it was time to get back to work.

It was late and there were only a few diners left in the restaurant when she returned.

She allowed her receptionist, Emma, to go home and took over at the desk.

About another half an hour and she reckoned the place would be empty and she could turn in. The front door opened. 'Sorry, we're closed,' she said regretfully and looked up.

For a moment she thought she was dreaming.

Antonio was standing in front of her. He looked as he

always looked, too handsome for words, and yet different in some way.

Maybe he wasn't really here; maybe she'd dreamt him up. Maybe she'd worked far too many hours and was hallucinating.

'Hello, Victoria.'

The deep Italian tones were real enough!

'What on earth are you doing here?' she whispered as the colour drained from her face.

'Now that's not a very welcoming line.' He admonished and gave her a half-smile. His manner was as arrogantly confident as always and yet... There was something different in the darkness of his eyes. 'Surely you can do a bit better than that?'

'I don't think I can,' she said stiffly. Yet every instinct was telling her to forget her pride and just go around the counter and fall into his arms. But she couldn't. He'd hurt her too much and she couldn't put herself through that again. And anyway, he was probably only here because he was at a loose end. 'I take it you are just passing through the city on business?'

He nodded. 'Yes, very important business.'

'It always is important business with you, isn't it?' She looked away from him and pretended to be continuing on with her work, putting the tabs for the remaining tables in order. But in reality she couldn't concentrate on anything except him.

'I found this, and needed to return it.' He placed a little red toy car down on the desk. It was the car that Nathan had loved so much that he'd run around with it clamped tightly in his hand all the time.

She looked at it in surprise and then raised her eyes to his.

'I found it in the lounge after you'd left and just the sight of it did something very strange to me.'

'What do you mean?' Her heart was starting to beat with hard uneven strokes against her ribs.

'I mean—it made me feel like someone had wrenched out my insides.' For a second he sounded angry. 'Is that clear enough for you? I'm saying that my house is unbearably quiet, that my life is unutterably lonely. And that I want you and Nathan to come home.'

She stared at him in astonishment. 'You miss Nathan?'

'Only every minute of every day.' He gave a depreciating shrug. 'Funny, isn't it? I'm the guy who didn't want children, and I thought I was being oh, so clever when I married you. And now look what you've done to me!' He raked a hand through the darkness of his hair impatiently. 'You've turned my life upside down! I used to be happy working long hours in the office. My home life was unimportant. And now...' He trailed off. 'Now I'm not happy anywhere.'

She didn't answer him; her mind was racing in circles of confusion. There was a part of her that was thrilled beyond belief that he was saying these things—this was good, *wasn't it*?

Berni came up to the desk and looked from one to the other of them in bafflement. They were just staring at each other across the counter, neither speaking.

'Is everything all right?' he asked.

Neither answered.

'Victoria, do you want me to take over here and lock up for you so that you can talk properly to Signor Cavelli?'

She shook her head uncertainly, but Antonio answered for her. 'Thanks, that would be appreciated.'

'Antonio, I—' But she didn't get a chance to say anything else because he was heading towards her with a look of determination in his eyes.

'We need to talk,' he said, reaching for her hand.

The touch of his skin against hers opened up so many memories in her heart...memories of his caresses, his kisses. The long hot nights of pleasure, entwined with him in satin sheets.

Fiercely she pulled away from him, trying to close the thoughts out. But she walked with him towards her apartment.

He was right—they did need to talk.

'So how is Nathan?' Antonio asked softly as they walked along the balcony towards the sliding glass doors.

'He's OK.' She shrugged. 'Fast asleep right now.' She didn't tell him that her son had missed him, too. She needed to tread carefully. How did she know that Antonio meant what he was saying? OK, maybe he missed Nathan now but it could just be a fleeting emotion. What if Antonio changed his mind? What if after a few months he no longer wanted them again?

What had really changed?

And he hadn't said anything about his feelings for her. Hadn't said he'd missed her, had never told her he loved her.

But of course he couldn't love her—if he had he wouldn't have let her go.

She dealt with Margaret as Antonio looked around.

'Do you want me the same time tomorrow night?' the woman asked, flicking a curious and appreciative glance towards the handsome Italian.

'Yes, please.' She tried to smile and to sound briskly businesslike.

She accompanied the woman to the front door and saw her out. And when she returned to the lounge it was empty.

She found Antonio in Nathan's nursery. He was putting the model car down beside him in the cot.

'So he sees it when he wakes up,' he told Victoria as he glanced over at her.

She nodded. For a moment they stood next to each other, looking down at the sleeping child, then he turned to her, his gaze sweeping over her, taking in the perfect curves of her body in the attractive blue dress, and the fact that she'd had her hair restyled into structured layers that suited her classical features. 'Your hair is lovely,' he said. 'But I'm glad you didn't have too much cut off.'

'I thought you didn't like it all loose and untidy.' She felt a little self-conscious for a moment. How was it he was always able to make her feel like that? she wondered angrily.

'Oh, I liked it all right—that was the problem. I liked it too much,' he said huskily. 'I liked your prim and proper ways and even your damn stubbornness.'

'I don't have prim and proper ways.' She arched her head up, and he smiled.

'I should have known I was in trouble the first time you looked at me like that.'

He reached out a hand and touched her chin, then traced his hand upwards along the side of her face. His eyes were on her lips.

'Don't, Antonio.' She stepped away from him.

'I want you and Nathan to come home with me, Victoria, and...' He trailed off suddenly as his gaze narrowed on her left hand. 'You're not wearing your wedding ring!'

'I didn't see the point.' Her voice trembled. 'Our marriage was just a business deal, and you said it was over.'

He said something in Italian, his eyes fierce. 'I shouldn't have let you walk away, Victoria. It was a big mistake.'

'No, it wasn't—it was how you felt!'

'I was fighting against how I felt, Victoria, trying to pretend that I was in control. I didn't want to fall in love with you.' He moved closer to her. 'But I did... And I'm sorry but I can't let you go without a fight! I've torn up the contract we made— it's in shreds in my office! *You are my wife, Victoria—you belong to me.*' The rough uneven edge to his voice tore into her. 'And I want you back!' His eyes were on her mouth. 'I want you now.'

Her body sizzled with fire as he reached for her, pulling her into his arms, crushing his lips against her. The kiss was filled with brutal angry need. 'I want you in a way that I swore I would never want anyone—with a deep aching need that fills every part of me.'

She looked up at him in wonder as he pulled back from her.

'I know I forced you into this marriage, Victoria,' he grated roughly. 'I know you can probably never feel the same way about me. And I've tried to stay away—tried to let you get on with your life and have your precious restaurant opening—but I can't bear it! I can't live without you. I want you in my bed. I want to have more children with you. I want to spend the rest of my days with you. Please be my wife.'

She swallowed hard on the emotional tears that wanted to rise. 'I can't believe that you are saying these things to me,' she whispered. 'Because I want to be your wife. I want to spend my days and nights with you. I want to have children with you. I love you, Antonio, with all my heart. I think I always have, right from the first moment I saw you.'

He looked at her and suddenly she could see the anger and the grim light of determination in his eyes turn to deep joy.

He really did love her, she thought wonderingly. This handsome gorgeous man was head over heels about her!

'I love you, Victoria Cavelli.' He said the words with such sincerity that it tore at her heart. 'And I want to spend the rest of my life with you.'

She smiled, her eyes shimmering with tears of happiness.

'Wait until your father hears that you want to settle down,' she said teasingly.

'I told him I was going to bring you home.'

'Oh, did you now! That was very confident! You know I can't just walk out on my restaurant and my staff—they mean a lot to me.'

'We will make sure the restaurant is run well. Promote that chef—what is he called?'

'Berni…'

He nodded.

'You always were very bossy,' she said with a smile. But she knew she would go back to Italy with him, knew it was where she belonged now. 'At least you are talking to your father!'

'Yes, thanks to you.' He smiled at her. 'He thinks you and Nathan are fantastic—and it's the only thing we've agreed on in years. Now do you think we can forget about my father and this restaurant and continue where we left off?' He didn't wait for her answer, just swept her up off her feet and into his arms to carry her through to the bedroom.

And suddenly nothing else mattered except the fact that they had found each other.

* * * * *

Harlequin Intrigue top author Delores Fossen presents
a brand-new series of breathtaking romantic suspense!
TEXAS MATERNITY: HOSTAGES
The first installment available May 2010:
THE BABY'S GUARDIAN

Shaw cursed and hooked his arm around Sabrina.

Despite the urgency that the deadly gunfire created, he tried to be careful with her, and he took the brunt of the fall when he pulled her to the ground. His shoulder hit hard, but he held on tight to his gun so that it wouldn't be jarred from his hand.

Shaw didn't stop there. He crawled over Sabrina, sheltering her pregnant belly with his body, and he came up ready to return fire.

This was obviously a situation he'd wanted to avoid at all cost. He didn't want his baby in the middle of a fight with these armed fugitives, but when they fired that shot, they'd left him no choice. Now, the trick was to get Sabrina safely out of there.

"Get down," someone on the SWAT team yelled from the roof of the adjacent building.

Shaw did. He dropped lower, covering Sabrina as best he could.

There was another shot, but this one came from a rifleman on the SWAT team. Shaw didn't look up, but he heard the sound of glass being blown apart.

The shots continued, all coming from his men, which meant it might be time to try to get Sabrina to better cover. Shaw glanced at the front of the building.

So that Sabrina's pregnant belly wouldn't be smashed against the ground, Shaw eased off her and moved her to a sitting position so that her back was against the brick wall. They were close. Too close. And face-to-face.

He found himself staring right into those sea-green eyes.

How will Shaw get Sabrina out?
Follow the daring rescue and the heartbreaking
aftermath in THE BABY'S GUARDIAN by Delores Fossen,
available May 2010 from Harlequin Intrigue.

HARLEQUIN *Presents*

Bestselling Harlequin Presents® author

Lynne Graham

introduces

VIRGIN ON HER WEDDING NIGHT

Valente Lorenzatto never forgave Caroline Hales's
abandonment of him at the altar. But now he's
made millions and claimed his aristocratic Venetian
birthright—and he's poised to get his revenge.
He'll ruin Caroline's family by buying out their
company and throwing them out of their mansion...
unless she agrees to give him the wedding night
she denied him five years ago....

**Available May 2010
from Harlequin Presents!**

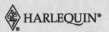
® HARLEQUIN®

INTRIGUE®

BESTSELLING
HARLEQUIN INTRIGUE® AUTHOR

DELORES
FOSSEN

PRESENTS AN ALL-NEW
THRILLING TRILOGY

TEXAS MATERNITY:
HOSTAGES

When masked gunmen take over the maternity ward
at a San Antonio hospital, local cops, FBI and the scared
mothers can't figure out any possible motive. Before
long, secrets are revealed, and a city that has been on
edge since the siege began learns the truth behind the
negotiations and must deal with the fallout.

LOOK FOR

THE BABY'S GUARDIAN, *May*
DEVASTATING DADDY, *June*
THE MOMMY MYSTERY, *July*

LARGER-PRINT BOOKS!

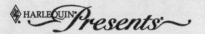